BUZZ AROUND THE TRACK

They Said It

"I don't like journalists and I don't like blondes.
If Tara Dalton wants a story, she'll have to go elsewhere."
—Adam Sanford

"Adam Sanford is reluctant to grant me an interview
because of his brother. He's afraid I'll ask questions about
Trey's dead-of-night flights to Mexico!"
—Tara Dalton

"There's no mystery here.
My trips to Mexico are my own private business
and I'd thank everyone else to butt out."
—Trey Sanford

"I know everyone thinks Gina is dead, but I've never
believed it. She was my baby. If someone is saying
she's still alive, we have to check it out."
—Patsy Grosso

KEN CASPER,

aka K.N. Casper, figures his writing career started back in the sixth grade when a teacher ordered him to write a "theme" explaining his misbehavior over the previous semester. To his teacher's chagrin, he enjoyed stringing just the right words together to justify his less-than-stellar performance. That's not to say he's been telling tall tales to get out of scrapes ever since, but…

Born and raised in New York City, Ken is now a transplanted Texan. He and Mary, his wife of thirty-plus years, own a horse farm in San Angelo. Along with their two dogs, six cats and eight horses—at last count!—they also board and breed horses, and Mary teaches English riding. She's a therapeutic riding instructor for the handicapped, as well.

Life is never dull. Their two granddaughters visit several times a year and feel right at home with the Casper menagerie. Grandpa and Mimi do everything they can to make sure their visits will be lifelong fond memories. After all, isn't that what grandparents are for?

You can keep up with Ken and his books on his Web site at www.kencasper.com.

NASCAR

SCANDALS AND SECRETS

Ken Casper

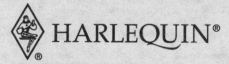

TORONTO • NEW YORK • LONDON
AMSTERDAM • PARIS • SYDNEY • HAMBURG
STOCKHOLM • ATHENS • TOKYO • MILAN • MADRID
PRAGUE • WARSAW • BUDAPEST • AUCKLAND

Recycling programs for this product may not exist in your area.

ISBN-13: 978-0-373-18519-1
ISBN-10:   0-373-18519-7

SCANDALS AND SECRETS

Copyright © 2009 by Harlequin Books S.A.

Kenneth Casper is acknowledged as the author of this work.

NASCAR® and the NASCAR Library Collection® are registered trademarks of the National Association for Stock Car Auto Racing, Inc.

This edition published by arrangement with Harlequin Books S.A.

® and TM are trademarks of the publisher. Trademarks indicated with ® are registered in the United States Patent and Trademark Office, the Canadian Trade Marks Office and in other countries.

www.eHarlequin.com

Printed in U.S.A.

Very Special Thanks

To my sister Florence, for all the good years

To my niece Diane, for being there when it mattered most

And to my good friend and fellow wordsmith Preston Darby,
for endless wisdom and inspiration

NASCAR HIDDEN LEGACIES

The Grossos

Dean Grosso
m.
Patsy Clark Grosso

Patsy's brother

Kent Grosso
(fiancée Tanya Wells)

Gina Grosso
(deceased)

Sophia Grosso
(fiancé Justin Murphy)

Patsy's cousin

Kent's agent

The Clarks

Andrew Clark
(divorced)

Garrett Clark ⑯
(Andrew's stepson)

Jake McMasters ⑧

Kane Ledger ⑦

The Cargills

Alan Cargill (widower)

Nathan Cargill ⑤

Dean's best friend

The Claytons

Steve Clayton ⑩

Mattie Clayton ⑭

Business Partner

Damon Tieri ⑪

The Branches

Maeve Branch
(div. Hilton Branch)
m.
Chuck Lawrence

Will Branch ②

Bart Branch

Penny Branch m.
Craig Lockhart

Sawyer Branch

THE FAMILIES AND THE CONNECTIONS

The Sanfords

Bobby Sanford
(deceased)
m.
Kath Sanford

— Adam Sanford ①

— Brent Sanford ⑫

— Trey Sanford ⑨

The Hunts

Dan Hunt
m.
Linda (Willard) Hunt
(deceased)

— Ethan Hunt ⑥

— Jared Hunt ⑮

— Hope Hunt ⑫

— Grace Hunt Winters ⑯
(widow of Todd Winters)

The Mathesons

Brady Matheson
(widower)
fiancée Julie-Anne Blake

— Chad Matheson ③

— Zack Matheson ⑬

— Trent Matheson
(fiancée Kelly Greenwood)

The Daltons

Buddy Dalton
m.
Shirley Dalton

— Mallory Dalton ④

— Tara Dalton ①

— Emma-Lea Dalton

CHAPTER ONE

TARA DALTON WAS beginning to panic. The whole point of her coming to the NASCAR Awards Banquet, aside from enjoying the company of the most famous stock car drivers in the world, was to arrange for later interviews with Dean Grosso, this year's winner of the NASCAR Sprint Cup Series championship, and Adam Sanford, the owner of Sanford Racing. She'd called in a lot of favors to be invited.

She'd arrived at the hotel early, specifically to set everything up for when the festivities ended. What she hadn't anticipated was that one of the four elevators would be out of commission and it would take her forever to reach the ballroom on the forty-third floor of the luxury hotel. By then dinner was already being served and she'd lost the opportunity to socialize with the people she'd hoped to sweet-talk.

Now the ritziest, glitziest night in NASCAR, the culmination of Champions Week, was over, people were making for the exits, and her mission remained unaccomplished.

"Come on," Tara urged her sister, Mallory, and started toward the dais at the front of the immense gilt-and-crystal ballroom.

"But everybody's leaving," Mallory objected.

"That's why we have to hurry. Before they get away."

Mallory looked back at the bottleneck at the doors. "I don't think that's going to be very soon."

She was right, of course, but Tara didn't think the middle

of an impatient crowd was the place to persuade her subjects
to give up precious vacation time to accommodate her.

Bucking the steady tide of people heading for the hallway
and the bank of still-operating elevators, Tara began to understand how a salmon must feel swimming upstream. Fortunately the people she wanted to talk to at the head table had
apparently decided not to fight the stampede and instead,
had commandeered two of the vacated round tables immediately below the dais, where they were sipping wine and
talking among themselves.

Tara glanced over her shoulder. Mallory had stopped—or
more likely, been stopped—to talk to a guy Tara didn't recognize. Mid-thirties, Tara guessed, and from what she could
see, not bad-looking, but then, Mallory had never had any
trouble attracting men.

"Mall," Tara called out.

Eyes keenly focused on the man, her sister raised a hand
and nodded in her direction. Tara knew she'd break away
eventually but she didn't want to wait. Patience had never
been one of her virtues. She spun back toward the head of
the room and moved on, practically at a run.

No one near the dais seemed to pay any attention to her—
except Adam Sanford, who was currently glancing her way.
Being noticed by a guy who was drop-dead gorgeous was
nice. Of course, Mallory had her back to him. Once he saw
her, Tara would cease to exist. Over the past ten years Mallory
had played wholesome girl-next-door roles on various TV
dramas. Recently she'd been picked up as a regular on *Racing
Hearts,* the New York-based TV soap opera about stock car
racing families. Now everyone in NASCAR seemed to recognize her.

Tara focused on her targets.

Dean Grosso and his wife, Patsy, were talking with Milo
Grosso, Dean's grandfather, and Kent, their son. A few feet

from them, Adam Sanford seemed engaged in a deep discussion with his brother, Trey, Sanford Racing's driver in the NASCAR Sprint Cup Series, and another heartthrob. Neither of them was smiling.

Tara was tempted to zero in on the two Sanford bachelors, but the Grosso family was closer and in her path.

"Come on, Milo," she heard Kent say to his great-grandfather. "Let's make tracks."

Dang. She didn't want them to escape, but by the time she made her way around a group of people who were blocking the aisle, Kent had escorted the elderly gentleman to a side door, held it for him, and they'd both disappeared through it.

Double dang. Convincing them to participate in her project might have been easier if she could have gotten them all together at one time, but that was probably being unrealistic. They could just as easily have ganged up on her to say no. The interviews she had in mind for Dean and Patsy would have to be separate and private, anyway, since there were things she wanted to discuss with them that were sensitive.

"Mr. Grosso," she called out above the din of the cleanup crew stacking dirty dishes into large tubs to be carted away to the kitchen. Dean turned in her direction.

She extended her hand. "First, I want to add my congratulations on your winning the NASCAR Sprint Cup championship."

He smiled in the practiced way of celebrities and met her eyes as they shook hands. She could see by his expression that he regarded her as just another fan, someone to be polite to.

"I think I've been to most of your races," she said, essentially confirming his impression, "at least in the last ten years. My parents have a motor home that they take to all the tracks. They think you're the best. So do I."

"Thank you."

"My name is Tara Dalton." When the name didn't elicit any response, she added, "I write books about sports figures."

"You wrote *Hoops and Happiness*," Patsy Grosso interjected from beside her husband.

Tara grinned. It was always a thrill when people recognized her. "Yes, I did."

"And *Rolling Uphill*. I cried my way through that book." Patsy looked up at her husband. "You remember it, the story about the boy in a wheelchair whose dream was to participate in a marathon." She turned back to Tara. "I couldn't put it down. Such an inspirational story, and you wrote it so touchingly."

"That's very kind of you."

"Of course. Great book," Dean agreed.

She doubted he'd read it, but the compliment was appreciated nonetheless. It had been an uplifting story but also an emotionally taxing one for her to write.

"I was hoping," she continued, "I might get a chance to talk to you tonight. I'm writing another book, this one about NASCAR moguls and legends. Naturally no account of NASCAR would be complete without mentioning the Grosso family. I called your office this week to set up an appointment with you, but your secretary said you weren't giving any interviews right now. I know this is your vacation time, and I hate to impose, but the truth is I'm on an extremely short deadline. I'm hoping you might be willing to make an exception and give me a couple of hours of your time."

NASCAR raced ten months out of the year. The two months between the end of one official season in mid November and the beginning of the next in early February was the only time racing families had to themselves. Tara recognized that imposing on that well-deserved hiatus, especially on such short notice, was poor form, but she had little choice.

"The person you really want to talk to about the early days of NASCAR is my grandfather, Milo," Dean reminded her. "He drove in the first NASCAR race on the sands of Daytona Beach, and he'd love to tell you all about it."

Milo Grosso and his wife, Juliana, still attended many NASCAR races. In his early nineties, he was remarkably steady on his feet and reputedly still sharp mentally. He loved to recount the scandal that had led to the animosity between the Grossos and Murphys, a half-century-old feud that Tara would have to discuss at least briefly in her book. It didn't seem likely the old gentleman would give her any new information, since he'd already told the tale so many times, but that was one of the fun parts about interviewing people. You never knew what they were going to say. Her goal tonight, however, was Dean and his wife, Patsy. They were the ones with the emotional story Tara hoped to explore, a story of heartbreak and perseverance, and perhaps now a story with a new, happier ending.

As part of her research process Tara received e-mail alerts from her search engine whenever key words or phrases she had specified were mentioned on the Internet. Among her list of names were the Grossos. Recently a bulletin board about missing and exploited children had introduced the name Gina Grosso. Apparently a newborn by that name had been stolen from a Nashville hospital three decades ago.

Dean and Patsy once lived in Nashville. A coincidence?

An exhaustive search of newspaper archives revealed that Dean and Patsy's baby daughter, Kent's twin sister, had disappeared from the hospital shortly after her birth and was never seen again. Wow!

Such an event must have had a profound effect on the young parents, yet they'd managed to keep it to themselves. Dean had been able to go on, build a successful racing career and, with Patsy, have a model home life. How they'd coped with losing a child in such a dramatic way would make an inspiring story, one that could help other grieving parents deal with similar tragedies. First, of course, Tara would have to convince them to talk about it—something they'd never done in public.

"Everybody's heard of Milo Grosso," Tara said with a smile. "I'm sorry I missed him tonight, and your son, but I must tell you my real interest in writing this book is getting your personal perspective on team building, especially since you've just bought Cargill Motorsports. Not only are you retiring as a NASCAR Sprint Cup champion, but you've become a team owner. I'd love to get your views on the two roles, what different leadership skills they require and how you plan to change Cargill-Grosso Racing."

Dean smiled modestly. "That's all very flattering, Ms. Dalton, but your questions are a bit premature. As a driver I'm old news, and as an owner I'm too new to give you any credible insights. Maybe you can check back with me in a year or so. By then I should have collected enough wisdom— or at least some stories—I can share with you." His expression was self-deprecating and playful, as well as, Tara felt, sincere.

"The person you ought to interview," Patsy informed her, "is our son. Kent's a NASCAR Sprint Cup winner, too, and he's competing against his own father. I'm sure he can give you a perspective nobody else can."

Tara certainly planned to talk to him at some future date about that and moving from Maximus Motorsports to join Cargill-Grosso, as well as the twin sister he'd lost. Her interest at the moment, however, centered exclusively on his parents. She could tell them specifically why, of course, but she didn't think this was the appropriate time or place. Tonight was a very special, very happy occasion. She didn't want to bring up sad memories. Not only did it have the potential to spoil the evening for them, but it would probably backfire on her.

"An excellent suggestion, Ms. Grosso," she said.

"Call me Patsy, please."

"Thank you." Tara looked around. "But where did they disappear to?"

"Left a few minutes ago," Patsy explained. "Nana—Milo's wife, Juliana—had gall bladder surgery recently. She'd fully recovered, but he still worries about leaving her alone. Kent arranged with the catering staff for them to take the service elevator downstairs, so his great-grandfather could avoid the crush outside in the hallway. Milo is remarkably spry for his age, but still…"

Tara smiled. "Smart move."

"Excuse me," Dean said to the two women, "I need to catch Nathan before he leaves." He slipped behind his wife. "I'll only be a minute," he told her.

Just then Mallory hurried up to Tara. Heads turned, as they always did when she entered a room or joined a group. It wasn't that she was dressed flamboyantly. Her fawn-colored full-length gown this evening, while stylish and elegant, wasn't nearly as extravagant as some of the outfits women had worn at this banquet. Yet, even with only minimal makeup and jewelry, her natural beauty and grace drew attention.

Tara made the introductions.

"I've seen you on *Racing Hearts,*" Patsy remarked. "I love your character…"

While the two women chatted about the popular soap, Tara used the opportunity to make her way over to where Adam and Trey Sanford were still in deep conversation.

"Wait a few days, until the heat is off," she heard Adam tell his younger brother, then he caught sight of her approach and immediately changed his tone. "So I thought I might get it for Mom for Christmas."

"She'll love it," Trey remarked smoothly, as if that was

what they had been talking about the whole time. The intense, almost troubled expressions on their faces didn't quite gel with a discussion of what to buy their mother for Christmas.

"I've got to run," Trey added, backing away. "I told my date we'd stop by her apartment for a minute on the way uptown so she can change clothes. See you at the party."

Trey turned and fled through the same side door Kent and his great-grandfather had taken, presumably to use the service elevator as well. Tara was surprised more people hadn't caught on and started using it, although she didn't imagine a woman in silk, satin and precious gems would be particularly thrilled at the prospect of standing next to soiled table linens and smelly garbage cans. After all, an unwritten reason for attending any banquet was to see and be seen.

"It must be getting crowded," Tara commented to Adam.

He regarded her as if he hadn't seen her before. So he was into playing games, disguising his interest behind a facade of cool indifference. Okay, Tara liked challenges, too. The only question was whether she should match his aloof tactics or engage him.

"What's getting crowded?" he asked.

"The service elevator. Isn't that where your brother just went? The Grossos used it a little while ago and now the Sanfords."

"Sanford, singular."

"If only the walls could talk."

He crooked an eyebrow. "About what?"

"Why, the interesting people who've ridden it. About the conversations exchanged in the few precious seconds between floors. Maybe even stolen kisses."

"You're a romantic," he remarked, his emerald-green eyes twinkling now as he looked her up and down unabashedly. "I don't believe we've met."

"We haven't." She stuck out her hand. "My name's Tara Dalton."

"Hello, Tara Dalton." He encased her hand warmly in his. "I'm—"

"Adam Sanford. Yes, I know."

If the gleam in those gorgeous eyes had indicated nonchalance initially, it signaled curiosity now. "I'm flattered that you recognized me."

There was no reason he should be. He was the owner of Sanford Racing, and his handsome face had been displayed in newspapers and magazines frequently enough to make it familiar to most NASCAR fans and a fair percentage of the general population, as well.

"Such modesty." She didn't try to disguise the note of mockery in her comment. Then she tilted her head to one side as if she'd just caught on. "Oh, are you supposed to be here incognito? Don't tell me. I've blown your cover."

He guffawed, a rich, deep rumble that was utterly masculine and definitely beguiling. "Are you here with someone?"

She almost replied, "My sister." Then thought again. He must have seen her with Mallory. Of course, he had no way of knowing they were sisters, and having seen her, why had he kept looking at Tara?

And why was she analyzing this to death? Enjoy the moment. Maybe he just preferred blondes. Whatever his motivation, he was moving fast.

"Hmm—" she put a finger to her cheek "—I don't imagine you think I'm too young to be out this late by myself, so it must be that you think I need a keeper."

Merriment played on his lips, but this time, instead of laughing, he did nothing, and that annoyed her. It was bad enough that she was making a fool of herself. He didn't have to take such delight in it.

"Actually, I'm a writer working on a project about legendary NASCAR families, and I was hoping I might set up an appointment with you for an interview. At your convenience, of course."

The sparkle in his green eyes turned as dark and hard as bottle glass, and the rapport they'd begun to develop disappeared. In place of the flirtatious interest she'd perceived earlier, she found what could best be described as disappointment.

"If you're interested in Sanford Racing, Ms. Dalton," he said in a monotone, "call my secretary during business hours. She'll be glad to set up a tour, although the place is pretty quiet this time of year. It might be better if you waited until closer to the start of the racing season. Things are really buzzing then." He took a short step back, establishing distance between them.

Tara gaped at him dumbfounded. Where was this abrupt hostility coming from?

"I don't need a tour," she retorted more stiffly than she'd intended and struggled to soften her tone. "I need an interview and your secretary said you wouldn't be available for one until late next month. The truth is, Mr. Sanford, I'm on a very short deadline for my book and really need to talk to you sooner than that."

He shrugged, as if helpless in the matter. "Leaving things to the last minute is always a gamble."

He walked away, leaving her limp and speechless.

CHAPTER TWO

"Something wrong?"

Adam turned to his right. "Hi, Nathan. No," he said untruthfully, "just antsy to get out of here." He forced a chuckle and picked up the glass of red wine he'd set down when he'd been talking to Trey. "It was fun, but now it's time to move on."

Like so many of those attending the NASCAR Awards Banquet, Adam was ambivalent about it. Recognizing people for their contributions to NASCAR and honoring those who had achieved difficult goals was important and the right thing to do, but sitting still in a tuxedo and starched, pleated shirt for hours of speeches and formalities wasn't his first choice for how to spend an evening with friends. He'd much rather join them around a barbecue pit, near a shimmering swimming pool or, better still, a sandy beach.

As for Tara Dalton, he wouldn't mind sharing a towel with her—if she weren't a journalist.

Nathan, too, was drinking red wine and took a sip from his glass. He seemed far more at ease in his monkey suit than Adam felt. "I'm ready to get out of here, too. You have another party to go to?"

Après-banquet parties were scattered all over the Big Apple, less formal gatherings where the men took off their ties, removed their cummerbunds and the women kicked off their spike heels. Some of the parties would last until dawn.

"We're hosting a team get-together at the Horseless Carriage in the Village," Adam told him.

Nathan chuckled. "Appropriate."

"Join us if you can."

"Ditto. We're at the Crystal Stair on Lennox Avenue."

Adam laughed. "Not exactly next door." Greenwich Village and Harlem were at opposite ends of Manhattan, miles apart. "I guess you'll be glad to get away from all this and return to Boston," he added.

A successful management consultant, cool, sophisticated Nathan Cargill had gone down to North Carolina to help his father finalize the business details of selling Cargill Motorsports to Dean and Patsy Grosso. Nathan followed NASCAR, could name names and quote statistics, but unlike his father he didn't seem wedded with the sport. In fact, Adam had the impression he could take it or leave it.

"I've enjoyed being part of the NASCAR world," Nathan confessed now. "More than I expected to, actually. As good as it'll be to get back home, I'll miss the roar of the crowd and the great people."

"You can still come to races."

"And I definitely will. I've always enjoyed being at the tracks, but now I feel more of a connection. Funny, isn't it? Dad's retiring from NASCAR, and I'm beginning to develop an attachment to it."

"How does he feel about retirement?"

"He's good. It was his decision, after all, one he says he's been contemplating for a while. I have to say, he's achieved something impressive with Cargill Motorsports. Ending his racing career as the owner of a championship team is something he can be justifiably proud of."

"I agree." Adam took a sip of his wine.

The truth was, despite the issues between them, he envied the Grossos. They were taking over a well-oiled team from

Alan Cargill, very different from the one Adam had inherited when his father, Wild Bobby Sanford, dropped dead of a heart attack fourteen years ago.

"And it's not like Dad's leaving it completely," Nathan went on. "I hooked him up as a part-time consultant with a PR firm in Boston. It'll be nice having him come up to visit several times a year. We've gotten close these past few months, closer than we've been since I was a kid and my mother was still alive. I didn't realize how much I'd missed him until I came down here and worked with him on a daily basis. We've made a good team. The PR job will be enough for him to keep his fingers in NASCAR, while giving him plenty of time to travel and do the other things he's been putting off for years. He hasn't publicly announced it yet, but he's planning to get married again. Mom's been gone almost twelve years now. He's been alone too long. For their honeymoon he's taking Joanna to Europe for a few months to do the grand tour. After that they're considering a trip to China."

"Good for him." Adam held up his nearly empty wineglass in a salute. "Sounds like a perfect setup for everyone concerned."

"Speaking of perfect…" Nathan murmured as he tilted his head toward a black-haired beauty.

The woman had broken away from the Grossos and joined Tara, who was standing by herself a few feet away. Tara still appeared stunned from her encounter with Adam. He'd overreacted and was tempted to go over and apologize. Not every female journalist was like Belinda Goddard, he reminded himself.

"Saw her on TV the other night," Nathan continued in a near whisper. "She was a guest on one of those late-night shows. Her name's Mallory Dalton. Apparently she's just joined that daytime soap about NASCAR. What's it called?"

"*Racing Hearts.*" Adam had never seen it, but he'd heard several of the women at work talking about it.

"I must say she looks even better in the flesh than she does on the screen, even a high-definition screen." Nathan nodded toward Tara. "I overheard the blonde introduce her to Dean and Patsy as her sister. They sure don't look much alike, do they?"

"They are different," Adam agreed.

In fact, they couldn't be more different. Mallory was petite, with raven-black hair, dark eyes and perfect features, the kind of beauty that lasted into old age. Tara was several inches taller, with blond hair and blue eyes. Maybe she didn't have her sister's classic beauty, but Adam found her intriguing, especially in that slinky black number she was wearing.

What was it about her that he found so appealing—that attracted him to her and at the same time made him irritable and downright unsociable?

Then it struck him. His ex-wife had been a blonde. Well, he scoffed, that was a bit of a stretch. Ashley had been platinum blond. Tara was, what did they call it? Dark blond? Still, Tara had two strikes against her: being a journalist and being a blonde.

He'd brushed her off. Now it was best to ignore her. Forget Tara Dalton.

Besides, after the way he'd treated her, she wasn't likely to come around, anyway. He could still see the shock in her pretty blue eyes and remembered the way her lips parted in stunned surprise at his unprovoked incivility. Well, if she stayed away, it would be worth it. He had no intention of opening up to her or any other hack out to make a buck at the expense of other people's lives and privacy.

One thing he'd learned the hard way. When you give a press conference, you stick to the details of racing and you answer only questions pertaining to racing. You don't engage in casual conversation or speculation with reporters and journalists. You certainly don't share your personal life with them.

In other words, you don't contribute to your own character assassination.

If Tara Dalton, blond journalist, wanted a story, she'd have to go elsewhere. There were plenty of other opportunities within the world of NASCAR. Looking at the crowd still standing at the far end of the room, waiting for the elevators, he could see half a dozen people whose adventures, good and bad, professional and private, would fill any number of volumes of trash talk.

"THAT ARROGANT, self-righteous SOB," Tara muttered as her sister joined her.

"What's the matter?" Mallory asked. Tara was always so in control, especially when she was working. She had a temper, to be sure, but her ability to stay focused was one of the things Mallory admired most about her younger sister.

"All I did was say I wanted to set up an appointment with him for an interview, and he turned into a pillar of salt, coarse salt. Okay," she conceded grudgingly, "maybe this isn't the best place to ask for an interview, but it's not like I was whipping out my steno pad and taking notes on the spot. I was requesting an appointment, that's all. What kind of owner turns down a chance for free publicity? I'm tempted to drop the Sanfords from the book and feature some other NASCAR family. Heaven knows there are enough of them. Maybe I should contact the Murphys for their side of the Grosso-Murphy feud. It's a legend in NASCAR, after all."

Mallory snickered. That was Tara, always with a plan. Close a door and she would find a window to crawl through.

"In fact…" Tara tapped her chin broodingly.

"I think you should."

"Except it's been done to death. Everybody knows the story of how Connor Murphy cheated Milo Grosso out of the cup sixty years ago, then got himself killed when he fell off or was forced off a mountain road riding his motorcycle at night. I'll discuss it briefly when I write about the Grossos, but I can't dwell on it. It's ancient history, especially now that the feud between the two families is over." Tara sniffed. "Nope. Whatever's going on at Sanford Racing is current, something that hasn't been covered before, something that must be important or they wouldn't be so secretive about it."

Mallory loved Tara's plan for her new project. She'd already written two successful books about sports figures. It was exciting to see her sister's name on racks in bookstores and supermarkets, even prominently displayed at airport newsstands. This next one, *Scandals and Secrets,* was going to be about legendary NASCAR families, the moguls and the legends. Two of them. The Grossos and the Sanfords. Sort of the good guys and the bad boys. Dean certainly fit the good-guy image—big family with a racing tradition, going back to NASCAR's founding, but with secrets in the closet. The Sanfords were the perfect bad boys. Not that Mallory knew anything negative about Adam, but his father had been the notorious Wild Bobby Sanford. Bobby held the NASCAR record for the most times suspended from racing. He'd gotten his name in the headlines for a variety of other things, too, including his death at the height of his career under circumstances that were less than savory. Adam had taken over the team and redeemed the family name—until four years ago, when his younger brother Brent, who appeared to be on his way to winning the NASCAR Sprint Cup Series championship, quit racing—some said he was forced to—because of an accusation of cheating. Since then the family-owned business had staked everything on the youngest brother, Trey. Tara told Mallory she was beginning to suspect he had a secret life, as well.

"How about Dean Grosso?" Mallory asked. "Were you able to make an appointment for an interview with him?"

"He turned me down, too. At least for now. He suggested I come back in a year, which would be fine if I didn't have a deadline in two months. Patsy suggested I focus my attention on their son, Kent, since he'll be joining them next season."

"Are you going to?" Mallory asked.

"It's an approach that might work if I had more time, but I don't. My outline's been submitted and approved by the publisher. I can't change it now. Besides, I'd still need to interview everybody in the family. Without Dean and Patsy...well, they're the ones who can tell me about Gina."

"Maybe you can get to them through Kent. Except I heard he's leaving for his wedding in the Caribbean tomorrow and won't be back until after New Year's."

Mallory peered at the back of the room. The crowd waiting to go had diminished considerably. "You ready to leave?"

"Hell, no. They're not getting rid of me this easily. Besides, Alan Cargill is still here. If I can persuade him to give me an interview now that he's sold his team—"

"You can sweet-talk him into lobbying Dean to talk to you."

"Exactly." Tara straightened her back. "Come on."

IT WOULD BE at least three hours before Grace Winters would fold her apron, go to her room, shower, stretch out in the hotel's king-size bed and pick up the mystery novel she'd left on her bedside table. She'd probably fall asleep before she got to turn more than two pages, but....

Her feet were killing her. A sixteen-hour workday was rough on the back, too, but it would all be worth it. After developing a reputation as one of the top chefs along the Eastern Seaboard, especially popular among NASCAR people, she had established her own catering company, Gourmet by Grace. They'd been constantly busy with private parties this past year, and she'd expected to make tons of money, but the costs of doing business in so many different locations, especially in cities like New York and Washington, had turned out to be even higher than anticipated. Clearly they needed to revise their business plan, but she'd leave that to her brother-in-law, Tony. The office was his domain. Hers was the kitchen.

Winning the catering contract for the NASCAR Awards Banquet in New York had been a real coup, since the hotel had its own well-reputed catering business. But NASCAR had specifically requested Gourmet by Grace and had been willing to pay a premium to the hotel for the privilege. Tonight's affair would put them firmly in the black for the year, and the compliments they'd received would undoubtedly bring more jobs in the next.

Wearing her immaculate white chef's hat, Grace stepped through the service door. She noted that several of the NASCAR people who had been sitting on the dais were now clustered around a couple of the round tables just below it, apparently not in a hurry to leave. As Grace approached them, Patsy Grosso came forward.

"Grace, the dinner tonight was absolutely perfect." She extended her hands, palms down, like an old friend. They'd met at other NASCAR functions that Grace and Tony had catered. The sincerity of Patsy's greeting made Grace completely forget her aching feet and tired back. She loved her work, even more when it was so warmly received.

"It was fabulous," Dean agreed.

Alan Cargill, his team owner—former team owner now—concurred and started to clap. Suddenly all those present were giving Grace a round of applause.

Grace had been applauded by dinner guests before, usually as part of a general recognition of people who had contributed to an event, but this spontaneous demonstration of appreciation brought tears to her eyes.

She smiled and thanked them, then added, "We're about to shut down the bar, but before we do, how about a last call?"

"I wouldn't mind a little more of this excellent merlot." Alan Cargill raised his nearly empty wineglass. "I have to admit all this festivity is making me just a bit nostalgic. This will be my last NASCAR banquet as an owner." He heaved his chest and let out a dramatic breath. "It's hard to believe."

Tony, wearing a black suit, white shirt and dark tie, came through the service door with a full bottle of the rich red wine, a white napkin under the neck, and topped off Alan's glass, while Grace went around with the chardonnay.

"How many of these banquets have you attended?" a blonde in a beautiful black dress asked Alan.

"Twenty-two as an owner, " he replied, "but as I was telling you earlier, Tara, I've been around auto racing forever. Started out in midgets in Tennessee more years ago than I care to remember. Shucks, at my age, I'm not sure I *can* remember."

There were a few polite snickers of amusement. He carried himself like a man in his twenties.

Nathan waved a hand. "Don't believe a word he says. There's nothing wrong with Dad's memory. I bet he can recite every grade I made in high school."

Alan looked at his son fondly. "If you're referring to that D in chemistry you received in your junior year… I've completely forgotten about it."

Everybody laughed.

"My birth father drove midgets in Tennessee," Grace said to him as she refilled Patsy's glass with the chardonnay. "Maybe you knew him. Jack Willard."

A brief moment elapsed, then a pleasant smile lit up the old man's face. "Jack Willard! I remember Jack. Didn't know him real well, but we did share the winner's podium a few times.

A great driver and a fierce competitor." He addressed the rest of the group. "Unfortunately Jack died in a highway accident. A terrible tragedy and a loss to the sport." He addressed Grace directly. "Your dad was a good man, a genuinely nice guy," he told her, and raised his glass in a salute.

The gesture touched her. She'd been an infant when her father died, so she had no memory of him, only the few faded photographs her mother had given her. As a little girl she'd looked at those pictures and imagined her handsome daddy playing with her and making her laugh, taking her to fun places and buying her pretty dresses, teaching her how to do things and praising her when she did them well. Maybe her childish imaginings were idealized, but Alan Cargill seemed to confirm they weren't overly so.

"Thank you," she said with a dry mouth. She held up the wine bottle. "Anyone else? I'll be glad to open another."

"Why don't you pour yourself a glass and join us for a few minutes?" Dean suggested.

She ought to go to the kitchen and supervise the cleanup. "Go ahead," Tony said with an encouraging smile. He pulled the cork on another bottle, brought it and a wineglass to her and poured. "I'll keep an eye on things in the back. You've been on your feet all day."

So had he, she wanted to protest, but sitting for a minute would be a welcome relief and would allow her to listen in on the conversations of these last guests, maybe learn a little more about the father she'd never known.

"Thank you, but just for a minute." She chuckled. "Any longer than that and I won't *want* to get up."

Everyone settled in for what promised to be a long wait. "I can tell you all kinds of stories about cheating," Alan said, apparently in response to an earlier question. "Some subtle, some ridiculously blatant." He snorted and looked at Dean. "Your granddaddy can tell you tales about cheating."

"And has. More times than I can count," Dean commented. "The feud that developed between the Grossos and the Murphys after Connor Murphy was accused of cheating Milo out of the championship was legendary. A truce between the two families had been *signed* only a few weeks earlier when Justin Murphy, grandson of the long-dead Connor, announced he was going to marry Sophia Grosso, Milo's great-grand-daughter, whether anyone liked it or not."

ALAN TOOK a sip from his refilled glass. There was reconcil-ing to be done, he decided, and this was as good a time as any to begin the process. He rose from his seat and went over to the table where Adam Sanford was sitting by himself. The relationship between the two men had been strained but civil the past four years, ever since Alan had reported the statement Mike Jones, Kent's gas man, made about Brent Sanford bribing him to sabotage Kent's car. The upshot was that Brent had quit NASCAR altogether, a move that had shocked every-body. It didn't seem possible for a man who had racing in his blood to just walk away from it—proof, some people decided, that he was guilty.

Alan stood over Adam but spoke loudly enough for the people at the neighboring table to hear him. "I was going to call you in the morning, but I think it's appropriate for me to say this in front of everybody."

Adam looked up at him, baffled and clearly on guard. Conversation had ceased.

"I owe you and your brother an apology. I've recently received information that indicates I may have been wrong about Brent being behind the fuel-contamination incident. I'm deeply sorry."

Adam looked more stunned than relieved as he climbed to his feet. "I don't understand."

"I don't want to go into detail now, but I think we might

be able to straighten this mess out once and for all. When are you returning to North Carolina?"

"I'm flying back first thing in the morning."

"Will you and Brent be available for lunch tomorrow? On me, of course. Turn One at noon?"

Turn One was a notoriously expensive restaurant in Charlotte that was patronized by owners, drivers and sponsors who wanted to impress one another.

"We'll be there," Adam said.

"Good." Alan returned to the other table where conversation had started up again. He only half listened to Dean and Patsy's plans for Cargill-Grosso Racing. Tomorrow's discussion would be difficult initially. The Sanford brothers had good reason to be resentful, but he felt certain they'd shake his hand at the end of the meal.

Absently he watched Grace Winters finish the small portion of wine she had allowed herself, rise, thank everyone for their compliments and courtesy and exit by the service door. A thought that had been eluding him surfaced. Grace claimed she was the daughter of Jack Willard, but hadn't Jack's baby daughter died in the same accident that killed him? A terrible tragedy. The baby had been only a few months old. Alan had attended the funeral service; Jack had been in a full-size dark-wood casket, his infant daughter in a small white one.

If that was true, Alan ruminated, how could Grace Winters be Jack Willard's daughter?

As conversations floated around him, Alan gazed at the door through which Grace had disappeared.

He shrugged. Maybe he really was getting old. He must be confusing Jack with someone else. Too bad Milo had already left. He'd remember. But Alan couldn't shake the notion from his head. He probably ought to check just to be sure, otherwise it would bug him all night, and he had every intention of thoroughly enjoying this last night as a NASCAR team owner—even if the team was no longer his.

"I'm going to make a phone call," he told his son. "Be back in a minute."

CHAPTER THREE

AFTER ALAN slipped out the service door to make his phone call, Tara looked around. Mallory was talking with Nathan Cargill. Their conversation seemed intense and personal, so Tara decided not to interrupt. The Grossos had decided to join what was left of the throng waiting for elevators. That left her and Adam standing on opposite sides of the round table, pretending to ignore each other.

The man had been pleasant enough when they first met. She'd enjoyed the spark of attraction, the initial banter. Then she'd asked him for an interview—an appointment for an interview—and he'd turned from nice guy to arrogant louse. She wondered why.

Anger, she'd learned from her father, was often a substitute for fear. So what did Mr. That's-What-You-Get-for-Procrastinating have to be afraid of?

She thought she might know. As with the Grossos, the Internet was her source of intelligence on the Sanfords.

Not Sanfords plural. Sanford singular. And not Adam, but Trey.

Tara kept tabs on several blogs, two of which featured the Sanfords. Their contributors were mostly women drooling over Adam or his younger brothers, but occasionally Tara picked up useful tidbits among the meandering comments, like the reports over the past three months that Trey had been making nighttime flights out of a small local airstrip and not returning until a night or two later.

Research further revealed that Trey owned his own small plane, and filed regular flight plans with the FAA identifying San Meloso as his destination. As far as she could tell, there was nothing in the small town on the west coast of Mexico, nothing special, anyway. It was dozens of miles from the nearest tourist resort, and the road to it was in bad shape. The information raised more questions than it answered.

Why, for example, would a NASCAR Sprint Cup Series driver make surreptitious trips to a remote spot in Mexico? Her mother once told her there were two rules about men. Look for the money, and cherchez la femme. Was Trey flying to San Meloso to meet a woman? There were any number of exclusive resorts that took pride in protecting their guests from outside intrusion while offering first-class accommodations in the bargain. So why San Meloso?

And why fly a small plane by himself when his brother Brent owned a charter service that could no doubt get him there faster and with the higher level of security of a larger multi-engine aircraft? Was there something "forbidden" about Trey's relationship? Had the family disapproved?

Finally, why did Trey fly from a small, remote airfield in the dead of night and return to that same isolated strip in the dark when there were more-established flying facilities available closer to home? Why fly at night at all? Daytime flying, especially in small planes, was safer. Again secrecy was the obvious answer, but why the secrecy? What—or who?—did Trey Sanford have to hide?

Perhaps there was a simple explanation for it all. If so, she wanted very much to hear it.

"Tell me, Mr. Sanford," she said, addressing Adam, "does the reason you're so reluctant to grant me an interview have anything to do with your brother? Are you afraid I'll ask questions about Trey's dead-of-night flights to Mexico?"

IT WAS A SUCKER PUNCH and it landed right in the solar plexus. Adam gaped at her for a moment, at least until he realized he was doing so, but by then it was too late. She'd drawn the reaction she'd wanted and put him in a spot where he didn't want to be—on the defensive—but it was his own damn fault. He shouldn't have had such a knee-jerk reaction to her telling him she was a writer. Not all writers were like investigative reporter Belinda Goddard, he reminded himself *again*. At least he assumed they weren't. The only way he was going to find out, however, and have any hope of controlling what Tara Dalton wrote, was to cooperate with her, or at least appear to.

"I hope you're not suggesting there's something sinister in my brother liking to fly at night," he said.

"Not at all," she replied cheerfully. "I imagine it's very romantic up there in the velvety black sky with only the twinkling stars to keep you company. Although, I must say, solitary romance doesn't strike me as very much fun, and frankly your brother doesn't strike me as the type. I could be wrong, of course." She smiled smugly.

Adam had to admire her tenacity. She was after an interview and she was willing to do just about anything to get it, including play games that came close to blackmail. Whether he wanted to admit it or not, he had a problem, and he would have to deal with it.

"Why are you so interested in me and Sanford Racing? You never did say."

"I would gladly have," she told him, "if you'd given me the chance. You seem to have a hair trigger, Mr. Sanford."

"I guess I did overreact a little," he admitted with a self-deprecating wave of his hand.

"A little?" She gave him a pouty, sidelong glance. "I asked if I could set up an appointment with you for an interview, and you insult me. A simple no would have been sufficient."

He sucked in a breath. He'd never liked being preached to or being told he was acting like an ass. "Would it have stopped you?"

She looked him straight in the eye. "No."

"Honest. I like that."

He studied her a moment. Her sister, Mallory, was almost too perfect, a china doll. Whereas he could imagine Tara enjoying the rough and tumble of...

Hmm, he'd better stay on track. "Do you think we can get past this?"

Her lips parted slightly as she gazed at him. With only the slightest twinkle in her pretty blue eyes, the expression would be...sexy as hell. He didn't like the effect it was having on him. Or maybe he did. Too much.

"Why don't we start," he said, "with you calling me Adam, instead of Mr. Sanford? There are several Mr. Sanfords, but there's just one of me."

A laugh burst out of her loud enough to turn heads. "No one will ever accuse you of being humble, Mr. Sanford. Okay, *Adam*, it's a deal." She thrust her hand out aggressively. "And to show you how conciliatory *I* can be, you may address me as Tara."

He couldn't help it. He grinned. He liked this woman. He liked her looks, liked the feel of her hand in his, and he liked her boldness. The woman had style.

"You were telling me why you are so interested in interviewing me," he reminded her.

"I'm writing a book about NASCAR. Inspirational stories about the moguls and legends of NASCAR. It wouldn't be complete without mentioning Sanford Racing."

"I can't argue with you about that. Who else are you including?"

"The Grossos, of course."

Adam nodded. "So Dean's agreed to an interview?" He was usually as reticent to play the media game as Adam was.

He saw her hesitate. "Well, not yet, but he will."

She'd fessed up. That surprised him. She could just as easily have said yes, used that as leverage to get him to agree, then used his agreement to talk Dean into an interview. Instead, she'd leveled with him. Maybe, unlike many journalists, she wasn't willing to say anything to achieve her goal after all.

"Then why should *I?*"

She didn't blink. "Because I'm going to write about you, *Adam,* whether you cooperate or not, and the only way you can hope to have any influence on what I say and how I say it is to play along with me."

He said he liked honesty and she'd just given him a spadeful. "You're a remarkable woman, Tara."

She grinned. "Thanks for the compliment."

He nodded. "I admire strength in a person, whatever form it may take. Okay, you've convinced me," he declared. "In my own self-interest, I hereby invite you to come to Sanford Racing next Wednesday at 10 a.m., at which time I will personally give you a tour of our facilities and answer your questions. Your *reasonable* questions," he emphasized.

He wasn't sure what he'd expected from her for his concession. Fawning gratitude? Objection to the four-day delay? A challenge, regarding the definition of *reasonable?*

"Thank you," she said simply. "Ten on Wednesday. I'll be there."

By then he'd have answers from Cargill about the accusations against Brent. That ought to take the pressure off her obsession with Trey.

Raising his wineglass to take a sip, he observed her over the rim. "I look forward to seeing you."

More than he should, more than he wanted to. But there was something about Tara Dalton that intrigued him.

SHE WAS DEFINITELY onto something, Tara decided as she stood facing him, watching him watch her. She enjoyed their banter, and she had the distinct impression he did, too, but it was a mere diversion, a sideshow. She was being granted an interview against his will because she had brought up his brother's clandestine trips to Mexico—which suggested he had something to hide. Then there were Alan Cargill's public remarks to Adam. What new information did Cargill have that might exonerate Brent Sanford from the sabotage charges that had never been officially brought against him? The story wouldn't be news by the time her book was published, but maybe she'd be able to put a more human face on the situation than the media were likely to.

She thought about Wednesday. By focusing on Brent's story, Adam might be hoping to steer her away from the subject of Trey's flights. Well, it wouldn't work.

"I WONDER WHAT'S taking Dad so long," Nathan Cargill said. He and Mallory had sauntered over to join Tara and Adam.

"Maybe he's having trouble with cell phone reception," Adam suggested. "I heard several people complain about not being able to get a decent connection on this side of the building."

Nathan checked his watch. "I'd better go find him. The party uptown will last all night, but the sooner we get there, the sooner we can leave. Dad isn't much of a night owl."

"I'll come with you." Mallory turned to her sister. "He's invited me to their team party in the Village."

"You're invited, too," Nathan told Tara.

She couldn't help glancing at Adam. It would have been

nice if he'd invited her to his team's shindig, but he hadn't. Just because he'd attended this banquet alone didn't mean he didn't have someone waiting for the "real" party. On the other hand, she consoled herself, Dean Grosso would be at the Cargill-Grosso affair. Now that she had persuaded Adam to do an interview, she might convince Dean to do the same.

"Thanks," she told Nathan. "I look forward to it."

"We'll meet you back here," Mallory called as she followed Nathan toward the service door.

NATHAN WAS GROWING concerned. It had been at least twenty minutes since his father had gone off to make his phone call, something he could have easily done in a corner of the ballroom. Nathan wondered why he felt a need for privacy.

The door he and Mallory went through led directly into a corridor that paralleled the long side of the ballroom. Narrower than the public hallways, it was obviously designed for utility, not ambience. Instead of the walls being dotted with stylish light sconces, fluorescent tubes ran along the center of the ceiling. The walls were painted rather than papered and didn't appear to have been touched up in a long time. The floor was asphalt-tiled, not carpeted. To the left, the corridor ended in swinging double doors with large, scarred, stainless-steel kick panels. Based on the noises emanating from behind them, a kitchen lay beyond.

At the corridor's other end, a single door led into what Nathan realized was the public lobby and the elevators. Just before it, at a right angle, was a slightly recessed doorway over which was a lighted exit sign. An emergency staircase, no doubt. Walking down forty-three floors to street level would challenge anyone.

Nathan turned left and was almost knocked down when the double doors flew open and a busboy pushing a metal cart exploded into the corridor.

"Elevator's at the other end, sir," the staffer informed him politely but with a tone of impatience.

"I'm looking for my father. He came through here to make a phone call."

The guy shrugged. "Maybe he went to the men's room. It's next to the elevators in the lobby."

"I should have thought of that," Nathan muttered to Mallory as he led her down the hall. The lobby was still mobbed, and people were grumbling about the poor elevator service. Nathan asked a few people he recognized if they'd seen his father. None of them had. Mallory waited outside while he checked the men's room. Alan wasn't there.

Nathan and Mallory again entered the service corridor. Halfway to the kitchen he stopped and faced her. "No need for you to come with me. Why don't you join your sister? As soon as I find Dad, I'll come and get you."

"I don't mind," she said. "Let's go."

She was right beside him as they approached the double doors to the kitchen—cautiously this time, in case someone else came flying out. Inside they found a madhouse that rang with the clamor of voices shouting over each other, dishes rattling as they rumbled along a conveyor belt into a steam-belching washer, the clang of pots and pans. The air was thick with lingering cooking odors and the sour stench of grease and detergent.

Nathan barely registered any of it.

Grace Winters came forward, her brows arched in surprise at their presence. "Can I help you?" Her tone sounded guardedly annoyed.

"I'm looking for my father."

"Last time I saw him was in the dining room with you."

Nathan explained about the phone call.

"He certainly wouldn't do it in here," she said, stating the obvious, "not in this racket."

"Kent Grosso and his great-grandfather used your service elevator," Mallory reminded her. "Could Mr. Cargill have left that way, too?"

Grace raised her shoulders slightly and canted her head. "Would he do that without telling you?" she asked Nathan. Before he had a chance to answer, she added, "Let's check." She rose on tiptoe and craned her neck, caught sight of her brother-in-law and motioned him over.

Tony Winters approached, wiping his hands on a white towel. He was medium height, with brown hair and brown eyes. "What's up?"

"Mr. Cargill is looking for his father. Have you seen him?"

Tony shook his head. "Only in the ballroom when we finished serving the wine. Maybe he went to the men's room."

"I've checked," Nathan said. "He's not there."

"I don't know, then. He hasn't been in here."

"He thought maybe his dad asked to use the service elevator like the Grossos," Grace explained.

"I'm sure I would have seen him," Tony replied, "but just to be sure…" He led them around a bank of ovens. The doors were open to show they were empty. Down a row of wire-rack shelves, they came to a kind of storeroom beside an elevator door.

"Sal," Tony addressed the short, middle-aged man standing outside it with a clipboard and pen in hand, "have any guests used the service elevator tonight?"

"Only Milo and Kent Grosso. That was about half an hour ago. Oh, yeah, Trey Sanford used it a few minutes later. Hadn't asked beforehand. Just said he was going to. I didn't see any reason why he couldn't."

"Anyone else?" Tony asked.

"Nah. I woulda seen. Been standing here all evening, checking things out. Except staff, no one else's used it." He smiled. "Enjoyed meeting the old gentleman, Milo. Nice guy.

Hope I'm as sharp as he is when I get to be that age. Says the secret is his wife's cooking. She must be some cook."

"Thanks, I appreciate your help." Nathan turned to Tony and Grace, who had followed. "Sorry to interrupt your routine. I'm sure you're anxious to get out of here."

"No trouble," Tony informed him. "Good luck finding him."

"You said he was going to make a phone call," Grace commented as they retraced their steps. "People have been complaining all night about lousy reception up here. Maybe he talked his way onto one of the guest elevators and went down to the lobby to make his call. Have you tried his cell? He might already be downstairs, waiting for you."

Nathan removed his cell phone from his jacket pocket. He'd turned it off before the ceremonies and forgotten about it. He powered it up but found no missed calls listed. He stabbed in his father's number, hit the connect button but received no response, not even a voice-mail prompt. "What could have happened to him?"

"I'm sure there's a very simple explanation," Mallory told him.

Nathan said nothing in reply. He was beginning to panic.

Tara and Adam watched them reenter the ballroom and approach.

"You find him?" she asked.

"No. I'm going to check the men's room one more time," Nathan announced and strode to the hallway doors.

Tara looked inquiringly at her sister.

"Nobody seems to have seen him," Mallory reported.

"That's strange," Adam said. "I don't know him all that well, but he doesn't strike me as the kind of person who would just go wandering off, especially when he knows people are waiting for him."

"I'm sure there's a perfectly reasonable explanation,"

Mallory repeated. "Maybe he agreed to meet someone and the other person was supposed to let Nathan know and forgot."

Suddenly the service door flew open with a bang to reveal Nathan. He stiff-armed it to stop it from hitting him after it bounced off the back wall.

"Someone call 911. I just found my father. I think he's dead."

CHAPTER FOUR

DETECTIVE FIRST CLASS Lucas Haines of NYPD Homicide clicked on his electronic notebook and reviewed the list of people currently assembled at the round table in the luxury hotel's grand ballroom.

Dean Grosso, retiring NASCAR driver, one of the honored guests at the awards banquet held earlier that night. He and his wife, Patsy, had just stepped out of the elevator on the ground floor and were walking through the lobby to their waiting limousine when they were stopped by a plainclothesman who informed them that their presence was requested upstairs. Dean had balked initially—they were on their way to a private party—then they were informed of the nature of the summons. Stone-faced, they'd returned to the forty-third floor without further protest.

Patsy Grosso, Dean's wife and business partner. They'd recently signed a multimillion-dollar contract with the decedent for the purchase of his racing team. She'd spoken little in subsequent interviews but had been holding her husband's hand since their arrival. She looked pale beneath her expertly applied cosmetics.

Nathan Cargill, single, son of the decedent. He'd found his father's body in the forty-third-floor stairwell, common to both the guest and service areas. He was answering the questions put to him, but just barely. In shock.

Tara Dalton, single, best-selling author of a couple of nonfiction books about sports figures and a guest at the awards banquet. She was writing a new book about NASCAR.

Mallory Dalton, single, Tara's sister, actress currently appearing in the NASCAR-based TV soap *Racing Hearts*. Referred to in theatrical circles as America's Sweetheart. She'd accompanied her sister to the dinner.

Adam Sanford, divorced, owner of Sanford Racing. He'd attended the banquet and hung around afterward to talk with other guests rather than stand in the lines waiting for elevators. He and the decedent had a long-standing dispute over the decedent's accusing Sanford's younger brother Brent of cheating. Shortly before he left the ballroom, the decedent had requested a meeting with Adam to resolve the issue, claiming within earshot of the others nearby that he had new information that might exonerate Brent. He and the others claimed to have no knowledge of what that information might be.

Grace Winters, widow, celebrity chef and owner of Gourmet by Grace. She'd catered the evening's banquet and shared a glass of wine with the guests after dinner, but had returned to the kitchen before the decedent had left the ballroom to make his phone call.

Tony Winters, single, Grace's brother-in-law and her business manager. He had been in and out of the ballroom all evening, supervising the gala event.

Detective Lucas Haines's investigative team was busy with NASCAR and hotel officials, identifying everyone who had attended the awards banquet in one capacity or another. Considering the number of celebrities who were already on the list, Lucas knew he'd be under enormous pressure to resolve the case quickly and with minimum inconvenience and embarrassment to the personages involved. That was fine with him. The rich and famous were often the most difficult to deal with.

The medical examiner approached, a young woman who,

Lucas knew, was at least ten years older than she looked. Rosita Schwartz was also one of the sharpest people he had ever worked with.

"Whaddaya got?" he asked, his New York accent in sharp contrast to the Southern drawls of many of the dinner guests he'd spoken to so far.

"Just finished a preliminary examination of the body," Rosie reported. "Cargill was stabbed once in the lower chest with a sharp instrument, most probably a large knife."

"Like a kitchen worker would have access to?" He didn't wait for an answer. "Have you found it?"

She nodded. "Yes to the first question. No to the second. Immediate cause of death was exsanguination."

"So he bled to death. How long would it have taken?"

"Based on the location and apparent direction of the wound, the murder weapon may have hit the aorta, in which case he would have bled out in a matter of seconds, no more than two minutes. Even if a physician had been present, I doubt he could have been saved. Too much blood loss too fast. I'll know more when I do the postmortem."

"Any signs of a struggle?" From his brief observation of the stairwell crime scene, Lucas guessed there couldn't have been much of one.

Rosie shook her head. "If there was, it was short. No obvious cuts or abrasions on the hands or face, though I might find something when I get him on the table. Any idea what he was doing there in the stairwell?"

"His son said he left the ballroom to make a phone call. The crime scene people haven't found a cell phone, though. His son insists he had one." Lucas rose. "One other thing. Man or woman?"

Rosie shrugged. "Odds are it was a man, but a woman, especially one skilled with a knife who knew where to aim, could have done it. It wouldn't have taken extraordinary strength. She would have to be at least as tall as he was, though, to get the right angle of insertion."

"Unless she was wearing high heels." Lucas glanced again at the notes he'd made on his electronic pad, slipped it back into the inside pocket of his suit coat and walked over to the table where the victim's son was sitting, looking drained and despondent. Finding a dead body was tough enough. Finding your own father in that condition was tougher still.

"Can you tell us how much longer we'll be here, Detective?" Patsy Grosso asked. The question wasn't challenging, Lucas noted, or complaining, just a request for information. "Our family—and the team—are expecting us." He knew they'd been headed to a private party. "We'd like to be able to tell them when—"

"Did he suffer?" Mallory interrupted. "Please say he didn't suffer."

What a beautiful woman, Lucas thought. He rarely watched television—except for sports, when he got a chance—but it hadn't come as a surprise when one of his female detectives told him Mallory Dalton was an actress, the newest member of the cast on a daytime soap opera about NASCAR. Her dark eyes were glassy with tears. She kept dabbing her nose with a tissue.

"He didn't." Lucas hoped that was true. He kept an eye on Nathan Cargill, the victim's son. Unless the guy was himself a damn good actor, the grief was genuine. "We'd like you all to let us take your fingerprints so we can use them for exclusion purposes. It's just routine. None of you are suspects."

"I don't mind," Patsy Grosso murmured.

"I have no objection," her husband added quietly. "Anything that will help find the bastard who did this."

"We appreciate your cooperation." Lucas glanced at the others. They, too, nodded their willingness to comply.

"If you go over to that table—" he pointed to the far corner where a technician with a police badge hanging from the breast pocket of his civilian suit had set up the fingerprinting equipment "—he'll take your prints and get necessary contact information from you. Then you're free to go."

"We were planning to return to North Carolina tomorrow morning," Dean Grosso informed him. "Is there any reason we can't?"

"No, sir. We know how to contact you if we have any further questions."

"What about the others?" Patsy asked. "There were five hundred people at the dinner tonight. What about them?"

"We'll be contacting all of them."

Dean met his gaze. "Alan Cargill was a good man, Detective, a decent human being, a friend. He didn't deserve this." With that, he placed his arm around his wife's waist and led her to the far table.

"Mr. Cargill," Lucas said, when Nathan started to rise, "may I have a few words with you?"

Nathan sat down again, heavily, like a man exhausted or in shock. Lucas figured he was probably both.

"I won't keep you long," Lucas promised, "but I do have a few questions I need to ask, and if you're up to it, I'd like to get them out of the way now. I realize this is a very difficult time for you—"

Nathan took a deep breath, nodded and exhaled. "What do you want to know, Detective? I'll give you whatever information I can."

"Did your father have any enemies, anyone who might wish him harm?"

Nathan shook his head. "No. He was not a controversial figure within NASCAR or outside of it. Everybody liked and respected him."

"What about the Sanfords? I understand your father had a long-standing dispute with them."

"Four years ago Dad was the messenger when Mike Jones, Kent Grosso's gas man, accused Brent Sanford of hiring him to contaminate Kent's fuel tank."

"Was it true?" Lucas asked.

"Brent adamantly denied it, but there was a sworn statement and photographic evidence to back up the charge. As a result Brent quit Sanford Racing and left NASCAR altogether. This evening, however, my father told Adam he had new information that indicated Brent might be innocent. They—Adam, Brent and my father—planned to meet tomorrow for lunch in Charlotte to discuss it."

"Was Brent Sanford here this evening?" Lucas asked.

"No, the youngest Sanford brother, Trey, was, though. He took over as driver for Sanford Racing in the NASCAR Sprint Cup Series, but Trey left shortly after Milo and Kent Grosso by the service elevator through the kitchen."

Lucas had already heard this, and it had been confirmed by a member of the kitchen staff who'd been posted near the elevator.

"This new information your father claimed to have, what was it, do you know?"

Nathan shook his head. "I have no idea. My father never said anything to me about it."

"Would he have?"

"Definitely. When my father reported the accusation that Kent's gas man had made against Brent, he started a chain of events that resulted in Brent's leaving NASCAR under a cloud of suspicion. My father didn't take that lightly. He loved the sport and the people in it. If Dad felt he had in any way been responsible for an injustice, he would want to correct it, and he would want to discuss it with me."

"Then why didn't he?" Lucas asked.

"My father was not a secretive man, Detective." Nathan pinched the bridge of his nose before continuing. "I can only assume he received whatever information he was referring to just before he got here and hadn't had time to tell me about it."

"And you have no idea what it might have been?"

"None whatsoever." Nathan was emphatic.

Lucas decided to take one more stab at the subject before dropping it—for the time being. "He didn't say anything to you about expecting a call from someone about this cheating controversy?"

Nathan closed his eyes for a second or two. He was obviously exhausted or, Lucas reminded himself, a good actor. He'd have to check to see if junior had any theatrical experience.

"He did not." Nathan gave a weary shake of the head.

"Is there anyone else who might know what this new information your father had is?"

"Maybe Dean or Patsy Grosso, but since he didn't get around to telling me, I doubt he had time to tell them, either."

"Your father was a very successful businessman, a multimillionaire. He must have made enemies over the years."

"I don't think success is a zero-sum game, Detective. Neither did my father. Just because someone is successful doesn't mean someone else has to fail." Nathan sighed. "Sorry. I'm sure you're not interested in economic theory. My father made his initial fortune many years ago, before I was born. Since then it's grown through sound, low-risk investments. As I'm sure you're aware, with his death there'll be a mandatory audit of his financial records. I'll be glad to furnish you a copy of the report when it's completed. You'll find that his portfolio is diversified, that he doesn't come close to having a controlling interest in any single corporation and doesn't…*didn't* sell short. He has…*had* no enemies, Detective."

"What happens to his money now?" Lucas asked, keeping an eye on the man.

Nathan snorted scornfully. "If you're suggesting I had a motive to kill my father, you're wrong. My father left me the house I grew up in and a standard, token amount for me to act as the executor of his estate. The bulk of his assets go to charity, or rather to a number of charities. I helped him choose most of them. If…when you delve deeper, you'll learn I have no fiduciary involvement in any of them."

"Are you his sole heir?"

Nathan nodded.

"Why didn't he leave his money to you?"

"In his previous will he did, but I told him I didn't want it. He made his money the old-fashioned way, Detective Haines. He worked hard, earned it and invested it wisely. I intend to do the same."

It sounded good, Lucas thought cynically, downright noble. Maybe too good to be true. Could the old man have written his son out of his will because of some disagreement? Lucas had no way of knowing the full value of Cargill's estate, but according to press reports, the Grossos recently purchased Cargill Motorsports for fifty million dollars cash.

"Do you have any idea who killed my father, Detective?"

"It's much too early to draw any conclusions," Lucas replied. "It may have been a robbery gone bad. His watch and cuff links were taken."

"What about his pen? He had a gold pen."

"Nobody mentioned a pen. I'll check." He tapped a note to himself on his notebook.

Nathan dragged a hand down his face. "His cuff links alone, with their two square-cut diamonds, were appraised at a quarter of a million dollars. The watch was also custom-made and valued at a hundred thousand dollars."

Again Lucas made a note. "We didn't find a wallet. Did he carry one, and if so, how much cash would he have had in it?"

"He carried a wallet in the inside right pocket of his jacket. Normally he'd have a couple of hundred dollars in it. Tonight it probably would have been closer to a thousand."

"Why so much?" Lucas asked.

"A single bottle of good champagne can easily cost a few hundred dollars, Detective."

Lucas nodded. Out of his league. Way out.

"He also carried a money clip in his left front pants pocket," Nathan continued. "He was a heavy tipper. Tonight, his last night as a NASCAR insider—" he paused at the words "—he would have been feeling especially generous, so it might have contained several hundred more."

Expensive jewelry and a lot of cash. Good reasons for robbery. Lucas made another note to himself to talk with other people to determine if the old guy was a discreet tipper or if he liked to flash money around.

"Thank you, Mr. Cargill. I'm sorry for your loss. Do you need a lift home? I can have someone drive you."

"My home is in Boston. My father lived in North Carolina. We…he and I are…were sharing rooms here in the hotel. You can find me in suite 2610 if you need me." He rose heavily to his feet.

"Oh, one more question, Mr. Cargill," Lucas said, "then I'll let you go. What do you think your father's reaction would have been to someone trying to rob him? Would he have put up a fight?"

Nathan wagged his head from side to side. "Absolutely not. Dad played golf, but I wouldn't call him an athletic man. Certainly not combative. He would have given a thief whatever he asked for. My father didn't believe in playing hero, not over mere possessions."

Mere possessions? "We've accounted for 350 thousand dollars in missing jewelry alone, Mr. Cargill," Lucas pointed out. "Not too many people would consider those mere possessions. I can assure you, people have been killed for a lot less."

The younger man shut his eyes for a moment. "Sorry, I didn't mean to sound like a rich snob." He exhaled. "My father would fight like hell over a piece of bread if it were to feed a hungry child. But at this point in his life, gold and diamonds were things he could replace if he had to. They weren't worth fighting over. Besides," he added, "they were all insured."

"DO YOU STILL WANT to go to the party down in the Village?" Mallory asked her sister. They'd moved away from the table where the police technician had taken their fingerprints.

Might be the perfect opportunity to get Dean and Patsy talking about Gina, Tara reminded herself, but she knew she couldn't bring herself to do it. Raising the subject of a child's kidnapping and death was bad enough. Stirring up those ugly memories on top of the murder of their former team owner and friend would be downright sadistic.

"I can't imagine anyone partying and dancing now with Alan Cargill…" Tara shook her head. "I just can't believe it. Less than two hours ago he was standing right here, talking with us, reminiscing, in such a happy mood, so jovial." Her voice saddened. "Who could do such a terrible thing, Mall? And why? That dear sweet man would never hurt a soul."

"I'm sure Dean Grosso will let you go to their party with him and Patsy," Adam said, coming up behind them. "It's their team now. They don't really have much of a choice about going. They'll have to at least make an appearance, bring people up to date on what's happened. Alan was well liked."

"Not by you and your brothers," Tara said without thinking.

Adam froze. His face was immobile, but Tara could see

the hurt in his eyes. It was a stupid and unkind thing for her to say. She needed to apologize. "I—"

"Four years ago my family and our business were practically destroyed by what Alan Cargill reported. Was he right to report it? Yes. Absolutely. He had an obligation to do it. I have…had no argument with him in that regard.

"Was he right in the way he handled it? Not in my opinion. Had he brought Jones's accusation to my attention first, instead of going directly to NASCAR officials, things might have worked out differently. I could have investigated it. He and I could have investigated it together.

"Instead, we were blindsided, and before Brent ever got a chance to defend himself the *media* and the fans were condemning him. My brother had to give up a lifelong dream, Tara, also a very lucrative career, I might add, because Alan Cargill decided it was too dangerous to let the accused know what he was accused of."

He must have realized he was getting angry because he stopped and closed his eyes, apparently to get his emotions under control.

Then he went on rhetorically, "Did he do it maliciously? I don't think so. He made a mistake, a serious one in my estimation, but that didn't make him an evil man or a bad person. In fact, I had a great deal of respect for him. I had even more for him this evening when he admitted to me in front of our peers that he might have made a mistake regarding Brent's involvement in sabotaging Kent Grosso's car."

"I'm sorry, Adam, I was out of line," Tara declared.

"I'm sorry, too." He didn't specify what he was sorry about. She decided not to press him. Everyone was tired and emotionally drained.

"If you do decide to go with Dean and Patsy, you won't have any trouble getting a cab home from the Village. If necessary, they can call one for you."

Tara shook her head. "I'm sure there will be other opportunities to talk to them. Imposing on them tonight, when they're still so raw…"

"I'm glad you feel that way," he said. "Most journalists…" He swallowed.

Tara clenched her jaw. "I'm not a journalist, Mr. Sanford, and I like to think I'm not a ghoul."

"My apologies." He reestablished eye contact. "I really didn't mean to be offensive. I was trying to give you a compliment. Ineptly, it seems. Again, I apologize." When her expression softened, he asked, "Do you think we can go back to Adam and Tara, or do I have to call you Ms. Dalton now as penance?"

She wanted to snap at him, partly because it irritated her that she was enjoying trading barbs with him and partly because she wasn't altogether sure he was being honest. "I guess my thick writer's hide is a little thin in spots right now."

She could see a retort forming on his lips and waited with anticipation for it, but he apparently reconsidered.

"I made a mistake earlier this evening in not inviting you and your sister to our team party in Harlem," he said. "At the risk of appearing opportunistic, may I extend it now—at least for a drink or two to help unwind? My car and driver will be at your disposal the entire time you're there to take you home whenever you want."

"You're still going to your party?" Mallory asked.

He raked his fingers through his hair. "I have a team that has spent an entire year giving their all. Alan Cargill was well-known and liked. I'm sure the news of his death will temper everyone's enjoyment this evening, but they still deserve to be feted for all the hard work they've put in over the past year. If you don't want to join us, I certainly understand and respect your decision. My offer of the car nevertheless stands. I can have my driver take you home and meet me uptown later."

Tara wasn't sure how to react. They'd traded insults. She wasn't keeping score, but she felt pretty sure they were about even. More importantly, she didn't feel offended by him. Actually, she wasn't sure how she felt about him. He was handsome as the devil, and as much as she liked his looks, she was beginning to like the man himself even more, a man who was willing to fight for his brother, even though that brother was now in disgrace.

What had Alan Cargill found out that would exonerate Brent Sanford?

"Thank you, Adam, but we can get a cab from here. I'm staying with my sister. It's not far."

He extended his hand to Mallory. "It's been a pleasure meeting you, Mallory. I hope we can meet again under more pleasant circumstances. I may have to start watching daytime TV."

She laughed. "If you do, please do it during ratings week." She continued to clasp his hand. "I've enjoyed meeting you, too."

He turned to Tara and suddenly the tension between them faded. At least the argumentative tension did. He held out his hand to her. She took it and felt warmth flow from his firm grip.

"Don't forget," he said. "Sanford Racing on Wednesday at ten."

"I'll be there."

"He's smooth, isn't he?" Mallory said a minute later as they stood in the hallway waiting for an elevator.

"I'm not sure if the word is *smooth* or *slick*." Tara impatiently pushed the down button again.

"He's awfully good-looking."

"And knows it."

Mallory grinned. "I think he's interested in you."

"What are you talking about?"

"I saw the way he looked at you. You can't tell me you didn't notice."

"Don't be ridiculous." But it was nice to hear.

CHAPTER FIVE

"WELL, OF COURSE, everyone was there." Mallory topped off her glass from the pitcher of margaritas on the coffee table and leaned back into the cushions of the couch. They were sitting in Tara's second-floor apartment in Charlotte. "It was the awards banquet, silly," Mallory reminded everyone needlessly. "Who would miss that?"

"We almost did," Tara reminded her. It was Monday afternoon. They'd flown back to Charlotte that morning. Mallory planned to spend the next few days with her sister while *Racing Hearts* taped several episodes of the soap at the track. In the meantime, she and Tara had gotten together with their good friends Becky Peters and Nicole Foster. Their families had had motor homes for years which they brought to most of the NASCAR races. The girls had been NASCAR infield buddies forever.

"If that darned elevator hadn't been on the fritz," Tara grumbled, "I could have gotten my interviews arranged early and we would have been out of there before…" She bit her lip.

"Before Alan, that sweet old man, was killed," Mallory finished for her. "Poor Nathan, finding him like that."

"What about Trey?" Becky asked.

Becky was a model and as beautiful as Mallory, except she was blond and blue-eyed, like Tara. Becky and Trey had had a few dates, but the occasions had never gone beyond dinner.

Past physical attraction and informed discussions of stock car racing, they didn't have much in common and had stopped seeing each other after a few months. By mutual agreement, according to Becky, though Tara had a feeling it was not as mutual as her friend claimed.

"He was there," Mallory assured her.

"But he left right after the ceremonies," Tara added. "Took the service elevator a few minutes after Milo and Kent Grosso. I don't know why he was in such a hurry." She thought about the incongruous snippets of the conversation she'd overheard between him and Adam. *Wait until the heat's off.* Then an allusion to a Christmas present for their mother. Didn't make any sense at the time, still didn't.

Nicole took a tiny sip of her drink. "I can't believe you two were witnesses to a murder." She nibbled a cube of pepper-jack cheese from the plate on the coffee table. This was a rare day off for her. She'd earned her medical degree, done two years' residency in orthopedics at Charlotte General and was now part of a consortium of physicians associated with the hospital. She was also doing public-service work.

"We didn't exactly see him get killed." Mallory shuddered when she realized what she had said. "He was in the stairwell and we were in the ballroom when it happened."

"What did the police say?" Becky asked. "Do they have any idea who did it or why?"

"Cops ask questions," Tara said. "They don't answer them. Best I can tell, they think it was a robbery gone bad."

"I still don't understand what he was doing in the stairwell," Mallory remarked. "If he wanted to make a private phone call, he could have done it anywhere. The ballroom had nearly cleared out by then. No one would have heard him if he'd kept his voice down."

"Everyone was complaining about the poor cell phone reception in the ballroom," Tara reminded her. "Maybe he went into the stairwell trying to find a better signal."

Nicole shrugged and picked up another piece of cheese, this time cheddar. "Or maybe he was just looking for privacy if there was someone in the hallway. Have you ever noticed how some people speak louder when they get on a phone, especially a cell phone?"

"She's right," Becky agreed. She hit the button on the blender in the middle of the coffee table to whip the margarita mix that had begun to separate. "Trey always insisted I didn't need a cell phone to call anyone because I yelled into it so loud I could be heard halfway around the world." She topped off her friends' glasses.

"Humph. Nice guy," Nicole muttered.

"He was probably right," Becky conceded with a shrug. "I do raise my voice when I use my cell."

"There are other fish in the sea," Mallory reminded her, then grinned. "You should have seen the way his brother was giving Tara the once over—" her dark brows bobbed up and down "—and twice over."

"Oh, so Adam has the hots for you, does he?" Nicole asked Tara with a gleam in her eye.

Tara laughed. She was darned if she was going to admit she liked the warm feeling she'd gotten when those gorgeous green eyes of his raked over her.

"LET ME SEE if I have this straight," Detective Lucas Haines said with barely controlled rage. He was sitting in the visitor's chair in the office of the hotel's chief of security. "In the past month you've had two muggings in this hotel, both involving the use of force with deadly weapons, and you didn't report either incident to the police?"

"Scarp" Scarpellito was in his late fifties with graying dark hair, a prominent nose and coal-black eyes. He'd been a cop some twenty years earlier, had demonstrated a problem with anger management and been strongly advised by his superiors that finding another line of work would be in his own best interest. His dedication to law enforcement had apparently not completely abated, however, and he'd decided to go into private security. There had been complaints of his manhandling a few people who'd sought unsolicited access to his clients, but the last such accusation had been more than ten years ago. Since then Scarp seemed to have brought his penchant for physical violence under control.

"The victims declined to file reports." Scarp offered a helpless shrug. "What was I supposed to do?"

"Obey the law, for one thing," Lucas declared flatly. "You realize I could charge you with conspiracy to cover up a crime, as well as being an accessory to it."

The security man's smile was as inviting as an alligator's. "But you won't."

He was right, of course. It would take more than a couple of low-level muggings involving uncooperative witnesses to get the DA's attention. The hotel didn't like the adverse publicity associated with guests being subjected to armed robbery on the premises. It therefore took pains to persuade the victims to accept the hotel's abject apology for any inconvenience they might have experienced, along with full, complete and undisputed reimbursement for any losses they might have incurred, as well as a generous voucher for their next stay at any of the mother company's chain of luxury establishments. A few thousand dollars of tax-deductible "consideration" was a small price to pay for goodwill.

Frustrated, Lucas clamped his jaw and got out his electronic notepad. "You're not going to be able to hide this incident, you know."

Another dramatic shrug. "We want to cooperate with the police in any way we can," Scarp asserted. "In exchange, we expect New York's finest to quickly catch the murderer, so we can assure the good people who come here for business and pleasure that they are completely safe."

There was no such thing as complete safety, and they both knew it. "Fill me in on the previous incidents," Lucas ordered him.

Obviously prepared for the request, Scarp opened the middle drawer of his desk and removed two yellow file folders. As Lucas read through them—they were well documented, he noted—the parallels to the current crime were unmistakable.

Both muggings had taken place following a banquet. The first had been a businessmen's luncheon that had lasted more than two hours. One of the attendees, a man in his late sixties, had returned to his room, where he found a man going through his belongings. The hotel guest demanded an explanation only to have his arm twisted behind his back and a knife poised at his throat. He gave the mugger his wallet and his watch, as well as a book of traveler's checks.

The intruder was never identified or found. The checks were cashed within minutes of being taken at a check-cashing storefront operation around the corner. Unfortunately the surveillance cameras weren't working that particular day, so the identity of the person passing the checks could not be ascertained.

"Pretty smooth operation," Lucas remarked as he closed the top folder and opened the one below it.

The second incident involved another catered affair, in this case an evening banquet at which considerable quantities of alcohol were consumed. The victim had returned to his room, a minute later answered a knock on the door, supposedly by housekeeping, and was immediately accosted by a knife-wielding woman who demanded his money and jewelry. The drunk attempted to take the knife away from her and was cut in the hand and chest in the process. The sight of his own blood convinced the hotel guest to cooperate. The thief got about three hundred dollars in cash and the knockoff watch the guy had purchased from a street vendor two days before for twenty bucks.

"Interesting," Lucas mused aloud. "Not many women go in for armed robbery, especially with a knife, and you'd expect a pro to be able to spot a knockoff."

Scarp snorted. "A sucker born every minute. Besides, some of those imitations are damn good, especially when they're new and seen in a dimly lit room."

"What does your gut tell you about this latest incident?" Lucas asked.

The man behind the desk elevated his beefy shoulders in a search-me gesture. "Fits the pattern, except for the stab instead of a slice, but we know the level of violence tends to escalate with some of these characters, especially when they don't get what they want. Assuming, of course, it's the same bad actor."

Except, in the case of Alan Cargill, this bad actor had netted a windfall in gold, diamonds and cash, probably without meeting any physical resistance. So why the violence? Was it gratuitous? A sudden compulsion on the part of the robber? Or…could the robbery have been an excuse for the murder? Which came first, the robbery or the murder?

Lucas rose. He considered advising the security chief that he ought to be more socially responsible about reporting crimes but decided to save his breath. Scarp already knew.

"Cargill's murder appears to be part of a random mugging," Lucas told his captain later that morning. "There've been a couple of unreported armed robberies of guests at the hotel in the past month. Both involved a knife as the weapon."

"Don't need a silencer for a knife," Captain Larson noted. "Easier to hide or explain away, too. Takes a different mindset, though, to cut someone than it does to shoot them from a distance."

"The interesting part," Lucas maintained, "is that the second knife-wielding robber was a woman."

Larson raised his eyebrows. "Any description?"

"Nothing useful. White, wavy blond hair, in her late twenties or early thirties, medium height, neither fat nor skinny."

"Oh, well, that narrows it down to only two or three million people in the metropolitan area—" Larson snickered "—assuming the hair color is for real and doesn't change."

"You know what the chances are of finding this mugger, Captain. How much time do you want me to spend on this case?"

"Check with the coroner," Larson directed him. "See if she's come up with anything about the weapon that might help narrow things down."

"I'm on my way."

"DO YOU THINK he'll go for it?" Patsy asked Tuesday afternoon as Dean pulled into Alan Cargill's driveway.

Nathan had been living in his father's sweeping, ten-year-old ranch-style house in a gated community near Mooresville for several months, ever since he'd come to North Carolina to help with the sale of Cargill Motorsports to the Grossos.

"I sure hope so," Dean replied, "but I honestly don't know. He was anxious to get back to Boston before his dad's death. Now…" He let the word trail.

They exited the SUV and walked up the path to the house's entry alcove. The place was professionally landscaped and pristinely maintained.

Nathan answered the door within a minute of Patsy ringing the bell. He was casually dressed in dark-green corduroy pants and a tan-and-red alpine sweater. His greeting was warm and friendly, but his eyes looked sunken and dull.

"Have you slept at all?" Patsy asked as she and Dean waited for him to close the door behind them.

"A little. It'll get better. Right now my mind keeps zeroing in on all the wrong things. Those last few minutes, what it must have been like for him. Wondering if he suffered. With time I'll remember happier events."

"He was a good man," Dean said. "He deserved better."

"Have you spoken with Joanna?" Patsy asked.

Alan had been discreet in his relationship with Joanna Crawford because by nature he was a private person and also because Joanna's kids didn't approve of her "cheating" on Daddy, though Daddy had been dead for nearly ten years. Joanna and Alan had been planning to get married in a few weeks, in spite of her children's objections.

"Every day," Nathan answered. "On the phone. Needless to say, she's a mess. As if losing my father weren't bad enough, her kids seem relieved he's out of the picture."

"That's horrible." Patsy was vehement. "We'll stop by later and see her."

"She'll appreciate that," Nathan said.

Entering the high-ceiling living room, they faced wide windows and sliding glass doors that opened onto a flagstone veranda and walled-in garden. To their left, a log fire crackled in the stone fireplace. Dean and Patsy accepted seats on one of the couches flanking the raised hearth while Nathan took a corner of the opposite couch and crossed one leg over the other.

"What can I do for you?" he asked wearily.

Patsy wondered if they might be moving too fast.

"First of all," Dean began, "we want you to know that we've decided to keep the name Cargill-Grosso Racing for the team—" they had originally planned to drop the Cargill name once the new season got under way "—in honor of your father."

"Thank you. He would be very pleased, as am I."

"And we're hoping," Dean continued, "you'll consider staying on as general manager for the next few months, at least until the beginning of the new season."

"Me?" Nathan's brows rose in surprise.

"In the time you've been here," Patsy explained, "you've completely immersed yourself in the business side of the operation. I don't know if your dad ever told you, but he was very proud of the way you've handled things, and so are we."

"Thank you."

"Over the next weeks and months," Dean hastened to add, "Patsy and I will have our hands full reorganizing the team around our son. It would be a tremendous favor to us if you would stick around."

It was obvious to Patsy that Nathan was interested. It was also apparent that the decision was not an easy one for him. He had his own business in Boston he'd already been away from for several months. Remaining a part of the world his father had so richly inhabited could make getting a sense of closure on his death even more difficult.

"I know you have other obligations," Dean went on. "Your consultancy firm up in Boston…"

"But your partner has been handling things since you've been down here," Patsy hastened to point out. "We're hoping a few more months' absence won't be a real problem."

"And of course there's the probate of your father's estate," Dean added. "With all your dad's records and interests located down here, I imagine it'll be easier to handle details from here rather than there."

"We don't expect you to do this gratis," Patsy emphasized.

Dean removed clipped papers from the manila envelope he'd brought with him. "We've taken the liberty of drawing up a contract for eight weeks with an option for extensions." He passed the sheaf of documents across the coffee table.

Nathan accepted them a little wide-eyed. Clearly he hadn't seen this coming.

"The terms of compensation are outlined on page three," Dean told him. "Everything is negotiable, and of course we don't expect an answer right away. We'll leave this with you to consider."

He and Patsy stood up.

"By the way," Dean remarked as they started toward the door, "we all heard your father tell Adam Sanford he had new information that indicated Brent was not behind the sabotaging of Kent's car four years ago. Do you have any idea what this new information was?"

Nathan shook his head. "The police asked the same question Friday night, and Adam came by yesterday to see if I knew. The answer is no. I have absolutely no idea what he was talking about. Dad never uttered a word about it to me."

"Strange," Patsy murmured. "I wonder what he could have learned." They reached the front door. "Nathan, I really hope you'll do this," she encouraged him in a manner that was almost maternal. "You'll be doing us a tremendous favor, and frankly I think it will be good for you, too. I can only try to imagine what you're going through. The loss of someone close is always hard, and for him to die so... If there's anything we can do to help, you know you have only to ask."

"Thank you," Nathan said as he opened the door, "for everything." He held up the papers he still clutched in his other hand. "Especially for this. I'll give you my decision in the next day or two." He shook their hands and saw them out.

ALL DAY SATURDAY, throughout Sunday, Monday and Tuesday, Adam kept thinking about Friday night. The awards banquet was memorable for three reasons: the first, of course, was the murder of Alan Cargill. Second, and far more important to Adam personally, was Alan's statement that he had new information that might exonerate Brent. Adam wished now he'd pressed Cargill, at least about the nature of the information, but he'd been so stunned and grateful for the man's apology that he'd been willing to wait a few more hours for the details. Unfortunately his son, Nathan, didn't know anything about it, or said he didn't.

The third life-altering event Friday night was meeting Tara Dalton. He wasn't immune to the beauty of her sister—Mallory was gorgeous—but Tara was the one whose image and personality kept flitting through his mind.

She had a sharp tongue and a quick wit, both of which he appreciated, but there was something more about her that captured his imagination. Not just one thing, either, he gradually concluded. The whole package. Forget her resemblance to Ashley. Other than their both being blondes, they didn't look anything alike. Ashley had fine, classic Nordic features, on a scale similar to Mallory's, whereas Tara had her own kind of appeal.

He would see her again tomorrow. At 10 a.m. For the interview he hadn't wanted to give her. Yet he couldn't stop himself from looking forward to it. Not the interview, but her visit, seeing her again, matching wits with her, because he knew without a doubt that they would be in each other's faces. He smiled at the prospect.

He kept replaying their meeting at the NASCAR banquet. Maybe not the most auspicious of introductions, he acknowledged, and he was worried about the real motivation behind her desire to interrogate him. Was it just to write a nice, inspiring book? He'd stayed up later than usual Sunday night reading *Rolling Uphill*. There was no question she had a way with words and had captured the emotion, pathos and the kind of joy that only comes from achieving a difficult goal. He knew something of that. He'd taken over Sanford Racing after his father's ignominious death, then later had to contend with the scandal surrounding Brent's suspected cheating. He couldn't put any of that on the same level as a young man with a physical handicap trying to achieve a goal that everyone agreed he was incapable of, but Adam understood perseverance and the mental fortitude to fight in the face of others' doubts.

There had been light moments Friday night, too. He liked Tara's persistence, her unwillingness to stop when she was confronted with a resounding *no!* A very interesting woman, one who posed a challenge. He'd always liked a challenge.

Adam's thoughts wandered back to his all-too-brief conversation with Alan. A few minutes later Alan had left to make a phone call. Had he actually made it? Who had he called and why was it so important for him to make the call just then? In spite of his anger at the way Alan had handled the cheating issue four years before, Adam respected the man for his honesty and integrity. On the whole he didn't consider the older team owner to be an impulsive or impatient man, so why had it been so important for him to make that phone call at once? He'd been willing to wait until the next day to discuss his change of opinion regarding Brent's culpability in the cheating scandal. Did it have anything to do with his need to make the phone call?

It was an angle, a possibility he and the police had not discussed. Maybe they should.

Adam got out the card the detective had handed him when he'd let them go Friday night with instructions that if they thought of anything, no matter how trivial it might seem, to call and let him know.

He dialed the number and was surprised when Detective Haines himself answered on the first ring.

"I just thought of something," Adam told him. "I'm not sure if it's significant, but…"

Five minutes later he had recounted the entire episode and the background that went with it. Haines asked him to repeat one or two points, indicated he was making notes, but when the conversation was over, Adam wasn't sure he'd been taken seriously. He'd received a polite thank-you but no enthusiasm.

CHAPTER SIX

SHE WAS LATE, and that irritated him. He'd been debating with himself for days about his impetuous invitation for her to come to the garage, but of course there was no way he could have ignored her, not after she'd brought up the subject of Trey's trips to Mexico. He didn't know how she'd found out, but that wasn't as important as the fact that she knew about them. He would do whatever it took to implement damage control.

Standing at his second-story office window, he saw an eye-dazzling mustard-yellow compact car rocket up the driveway, skid around a corner and bounce to a stop in one of the parking spaces. The lot was empty this time of year.

He considered going downstairs to meet her, but he didn't want to appear too eager.

"Ms. Dalton is here," his secretary announced from the doorway before he had a chance to ensconce himself behind his desk.

"Sorry I'm late," Tara huffed, as she stepped around the older woman and came directly toward him. The secretary crooked an amused eyebrow and withdrew. "I started out early," Tara prattled on, "but there was a slowdown for construction on 27. I wanted to call ahead to let you know I would be delayed, but I couldn't get a signal on my cell."

Adam felt like a teacher in high school listening to a tale of the-dog-ate-my-homework. He laughed in spite of himself and glanced at the clock on the desk.

"Only a few minutes late," he noted. Twenty actually.

She was wearing hip-hugging jeans and a light blue sweater that clung to her curves even more tantalizingly than the classy black dress she'd been wearing Friday night. Classy was nice, but this…this was even better.

"Shall we get started?" He pointed to the satchel she was lugging in her right hand. "You can leave that here if you like and pick it up later."

"Do you mind if I record our discussion?" She deposited the bag on the guest chair and dipped into its depths, coming up with a handheld digital recorder. "It's easier and less intrusive than having to stop all the time to take notes and then try to decipher them afterward."

He wanted to say no. It was like having your mother-in-law eavesdropping on your conversation. On the other hand, knowing his every word was being recorded might keep him from making statements he would later regret—and from being misquoted. "No problem."

They took the elevator down to the lobby, where he pointed out major items of interest, like the car his father had driven the year he won the NASCAR Sprint Cup Series championship.

"He died the following year, didn't he?" she asked.

"Actually it was two years later. I had one semester to go before graduation from college. Mom took over until I was able to."

"Must have been tough." She poked her head under the car's raised hood to examine the engine.

He wondered if she had any idea what she was looking at. He also wondered if it was the reference to his father's death or the mantel of ownership that Tara thought was tough. For him or for his mother? The general statement applied to both, though in retrospect his mother had handled both situations with her usual diligence and dignity.

"You do what you have to do," he informed her. "Dad had built a good team. It was mostly a matter of just following through." That wasn't completely true, but it was close enough. Wild Bobby had been a smooth talker. The other half of his personality, however, had been his propensity for manipulation and occasional intimidation. After he died Adam tried to approach problems with more consistency and professionalism. The team garnered more wins and awards in the ten years after Bobby's death than the ten before—until Brent was accused of sabotage.

"Did you ever want to be a driver?" Tara asked.

"I did drive short track for a while," he admitted, "until I realized I didn't have what it took. I was competent, but racing is about being better than that."

"Were you disappointed?" she asked.

He shrugged. "None of us likes to admit we can't do something or that we can't do it well—" especially when your father was a champion and everybody assumed you would be, too "—but as the saying goes, the truth shall set you free."

He squired her over to a display case and started filling her in with tidbits of history and technical information as they went along, not telling her anything she probably hadn't already learned from basic research or that she couldn't have picked up from reading the information cards prominently on display.

From there he led her into the working area of the garage, which could only be accessed with a key card. Since this was between seasons and the holidays were approaching, only a few people were around. The place was mournful in its silence. No engines roared. No hammers pounded. Adam directed her to Trey's car, No. 483.

"We're going to take the NASCAR Sprint Cup championship next year," he announced with utter confidence. He waved a hand, inviting her to inspect the vehicle.

"You're running just one car, one driver?" She strolled

around the decal-covered vehicle, which was missing several essential components, including two fenders and the engine.

"One car in the NASCAR Sprint Cup Series," he confirmed. "Shelly Green is racing in the NASCAR Nationwide Series and doing very well," he added.

"Are you considering moving her up?" Tara stuck her head under the open hood.

Adam crossed his arms over his chest and raised a hand to his chin as he observed Tara bending over the radiator. "We always like to keep our options open."

"Of course, she's a woman," Tara said offhandedly, her voice muffled by her posture. She pulled back and straightened. "There aren't any women in the series." She threw him a taunting smile.

He smiled back. "I hope you're not suggesting Sanford Racing is sexist."

"I didn't say that." She made another circuit of the incomplete stock car.

Hmm. Defensive. He liked that. "If we were, Shelly wouldn't be racing in the NASCAR Nationwide Series, but she is. Ipso facto."

"Ipso facto?" Her eyes filled with amusement as she stared at him across the roof of the car.

"Latin," he explained. "It means, *Well, duh!*"

She laughed, her whole face lighting up. "I assume that's not a literal translation."

He grinned, definitely enjoying the moment. "I think it's called a loose interpretation."

She chuckled again, a bubbly sound that stirred his heart.

"Do you have anyone specific in mind for the NASCAR Sprint Cup Series this coming season?" she asked a moment later. "Besides Trey, I mean."

"No one we're ready to identify at this time." He hoped that was ambiguous enough. It could mean they did and weren't ready to announce it, or that they didn't have anyone, which was the case.

"How about Brent? Any chance of him coming back?"

He should have been prepared for the question and had to fight an urge to frown. It had been four years since his brother hung up his helmet and walked away from NASCAR. Adam had wanted him to fight the allegation that he had hired Mike Jones to sabotage Kent Grosso's car, fight it all the way to court, if necessary, but Brent had refused. Instead of defending himself, he'd turned his back on the livelihood and way of life that had been his heritage, the sport that he'd loved and competed in with all his heart for nearly fifteen years. At thirty-one he'd traded a driver's steering wheel for a pilot's yoke and now owned and operated a successful charter-flight service that ferried the Sanford team and several other owners and sponsors all over the country.

In the sudden silence Adam realized Tara was staring at him. "I'm not going to speculate on hypotheticals," he stated.

She studied him for another moment, then stuck her head through the driver's-side window and examined the utilitarian dashboard. Pulling out and straightening, she said, "Of course he would first have to clear himself of the charges against him."

"If you recall," Adam countered, "no formal criminal or civil charges were ever brought against him. Alan Cargill admitted the other night that he had new information and he might have been wrong in accusing Brent."

"Do you have any idea what it was?"

"I wish I did."

"You must have some idea."

"I just told you I don't."

"What do you think it might be?" she persisted. "What are the possibilities?"

This was skirting much too close to his interview with Belinda Goddard. Belinda had trapped him into what-if rumors and alternative theories, then twisted them just enough to make him look like someone he wasn't. Not again.

"No comment."

"Surely you have some idea." She just wouldn't give up.

Adam could feel heat suffusing his cheeks. He started to respond, then realized he would be doing exactly what she wanted him to do, rising to the bait.

He closed his mouth, drew in a breath. "No comment, Tara. That's English for—" he forced a tight smile "—I'm not going to talk about it." He waved an arm. "Shall we move on?"

He circled the car and moved toward the fabrication shop. No one was there today, but he could show her around and explain what was done. After that he would take her to the engine shop. They'd been testing an engine earlier. Perhaps they'd be revving it up again.

"But it's important," she insisted, struggling to keep up with his long-legged pace. "Sanford Racing's integrity and reputation are inextricably tied to what he did—" she paused "—or didn't do."

Adam stopped short. She almost bumped into him.

"Please turn off your recorder," he requested firmly.

"I'm just asking questions anyone would ask," she pleaded.

"Please turn off your recorder," he repeated.

"I don't understand."

"I'll ask you one more time, Ms. Dalton. Please turn off your recorder."

She stared at him, worried now, even frightened by his intense gaze. With shaky fingers, she lifted the small compact device, pressed a button, and the green light went out.

"Do you have any more recording devices on you?" he asked.

She glared at him, angry now at the implication. "No, I do not." She puffed out her chest. "What the hell's going on, Adam?"

"I don't like the direction this interview is taking."

"Ipso facto," she snapped back, but without a hint of humor.

He hoped his tiny grin didn't show.

"How many times do I have to say I don't want to discuss a subject before you believe me? I've told you several times now that I have nothing more to say on the subject of Alan Cargill's remark the other night. When are you going to accept that? If roles were reversed you'd accuse me of bullying."

That almost brought a smile. He saw it, the twitch at the corners of her mouth before she caught herself.

"Why are you so gun-shy about questions concerning your brothers?" she demanded, apparently subscribing to the theory that the best defense was a good offense. "I'm not asking anything that hasn't been asked before and won't be asked again."

"See, you've finally figured it out. The questions have been asked and answered. Asking them again isn't going to change the truth or validity of the answers, whether you like them or not. Problems get solved with facts, not idle speculation. I refuse to allow myself to get caught up in guessing games."

"Then don't," she retorted. "But you don't have to turn all high and mighty just because the questions are asked."

"And you don't have to challenge answers like a prosecuting attorney." He was making a fool of himself. Again. What was it about this woman that brought out the worst in him? "I don't want to be recorded."

"Okay, fine," she enunciated slowly, "then we won't record. But I have to remind you, Adam, that you invited me here because you wanted me to see Sanford Racing through your eyes, so how about we get on with the tour? Or I can leave and you can sulk by yourself."

He raised his brows. "My, your powers of persuasion are impressive," he said, dripping sarcasm.

"Sorry," she mumbled, looking away, momentarily embarrassed. Seemed like he'd gotten under her skin, too. "That was uncalled for."

Except maybe it wasn't. There was no question that he was sensitive when it came to his brothers, and she was right about why he'd invited her here.

He drew himself up, unclamped his jaw. "I'm sorry, too. I guess you've figured out I'm a bit thin-skinned about my brothers. Family is important to me, Tara. We've been hurt by facts, like my father's death, but we've been more harmed by implication and innuendo. Brent's situation comes to mind. I can't change facts, especially those I'm not responsible for, but I can do my best not to contribute to idle speculation and rumor."

She faced him. "Do you realize you're doing to me exactly what you say you want to prevent me from doing to you?"

He stared at her. "What's that?"

"You're assuming things about me, assuming I have the goals and mentality of a tabloid journalist, without any foundation in fact."

"I'm drawing a conclusion," he intoned archly, "based on past experience."

"Not with me!"

From her perspective she was right, he realized, but so was he. He proceeded in silence to the next area of the vast garage.

"This is the fabrication room," he resumed in authoritative tour-guide mode.

Leading her to a backup car that was under construction, he explained how the body of each vehicle in NASCAR was handmade from the chassis up.

"Aren't you going to take any notes?" he asked about halfway through his pitch.

"No need."

"You have a photographic memory?" At this point he wasn't sure if there was anything about this woman that would surprise him.

"No," she said.

"Then why—"

"Because none of this is important. I can get it on TV, or I can order books off the Internet that will explain it all to me with tables and charts."

He shoved his hands into his pockets and slouched against a workbench. "Now it's my turn to ask what the hell's going on. If you don't want a tour, why are you here?"

"I'm interested in you."

His heart stopped, then restarted with a thump. "Excuse me?"

"Remember what I told you the premise of my book is? Moguls and legends of NASCAR. I'm not writing a treatise on race cars, Adam. I'm writing about the *people* who are associated with race cars and racing. Dean Grosso as a driver and now an owner. You as an owner. I'm much more interested in listening to the inflection in your voice, the passion you evoke when you talk about your team, than I am about the mechanics of getting to Victory Lane."

For once he didn't have a smart comeback. He was also quickly discovering that keeping up with, much less staying a step ahead of this woman wasn't easy. She was studying him again. He wasn't sure if he liked it or feared it. He was sure it raised his pulse rate.

"Is there a soda machine around somewhere?" she asked. "I'm thirsty."

"Come on." He placed his hand at the small of her back and steered her toward the main building. "I have soft drinks up in my office."

His mind was a-jumble as they walked side by side. He

caught her fleeting scent, spicy rather than sweet. Yes, that suited her. In an alcove off his secretary's office was a tiny snack area with a small refrigerator, a microwave oven and a stainless-steel sink.

"What's your pleasure?" He opened the fridge door, displaying a variety of sodas, juices, bottled water and sports drinks. She selected a juice. He opted for a sports drink. They migrated into his office.

"You've been badly burned by the press, haven't you?" she asked after taking a healthy swallow from her bottle and sitting down in the chair he indicated in the conversation pit across from his desk.

"Very perceptive." He instantly regretted the cynical tone. "I had an unpleasant experience that ultimately cost me a great deal of money—" though the money wasn't the primary concern. "That's why I refuse to speculate."

She listened, waited a minute before responding. "I'm sorry," she finally said. "Trusting someone and then having that trust betrayed is hard to overcome."

She was smarter than he had given her credit for and he resolved not to underestimate her again. He also wondered if she might be speaking from personal experience.

"First, Adam, I'm not the press or the media. I write books, not articles. Well, an occasional article but not a gossip column. *Books,* not exposés. I'm not interested in trashing anyone. What I am interested in is the human side of your world."

He crossed an ankle over the other knee and leaned back into the upholstered chair. "With all due respect, Tara, what you call human interest I call none of your business."

She paused to consider. "Fair enough. It may surprise you, but I do believe in the right to privacy."

"Then why are you here? I made it perfectly clear from the outset that I'm not interested in being in your book."

"Because I'm hoping to earn your trust, develop a certain level of collaboration with you and write an inspirational story of perseverance against obstacles, against the odds."

He was tempted to say she must be desperate if she was looking for inspiration from him. "And the alternative? I don't suppose I can convince you to write about someone else?"

She shook her head. "I already have a contract for this book, and it includes you."

"That was presumptuous of you."

She settled more deeply into her chair, too, and crossed one long leg over the other. With untroubled confidence she said, "Like it or not, Adam, you are a public figure. That allows me to write about you without your permission, even against your expressed wishes. You're in the public domain. As long as I don't state as fact something that is provably untrue with the intent to harm, I can say anything I want about you. I would prefer to have your cooperation, but I can meet my goals and deadlines without it."

"It's something of a dilemma, isn't it? You blackmail me—" he held up a hand to forestall her objection "—into cooperating by essentially telling me you'll trash my family and me if I don't, and I bribe you with fawning cooperation in the hope that you won't."

She started to rise. "I'd better go," she muttered dully, un mistakably offended.

As she'd noted, his purpose for inviting her here was to give her his slant on events. The last thing he could afford was for her to start speculating about Trey's trips to Mexico. If the truth came out about them, it could mean the end of Sanford Racing. He shifted uncomfortably in his seat. His added awareness that she looked sexy as hell in that sweater didn't help.

"Quitter," he mumbled.

Momentarily stunned, she resettled into the chair and stared at him.

"What do you want to know?" he asked quietly.

Confused by the ping-pong of events, she said, "Let's get the hot-button issue over with first. Why does Trey fly to Mexico in the dead of night?"

Adam forced an ironic laugh. At least he'd been able to prepare himself for this question.

"It's not nearly as mysterious or as sinister as you make it sound. He goes there to get away—" Adam saw her skepticism "—to visit with friends and go fishing from the little seacoast town of San Meloso, where he doesn't have to worry about a bunch of fans and paparazzi hounding him."

She wasn't buying it, he sensed, but she wasn't willing to call him a liar yet, either.

"Ever heard of Roberto Castillo?" he asked.

"The open-wheel driver?"

Adam nodded. "He's seriously considering competing in NASCAR. He and Trey have been discussing it for months."

"Are you planning to add him to the Sanford team?"

"It's under consideration," he told her, though it wasn't quite true. Not because he didn't want to, but because at this point he couldn't meet Castillo's financial demands, and he couldn't afford to run two cars in the NASCAR Sprint Cup Series.

"Seems to me if you were going to do it," Tara countered, "you would at least have signed a letter of intent by now and would be broadcasting it to the world. Signing up an open-wheel driver would be a big coup. As for fishing…" She snorted. "None of this explains his flying out and coming back in the dead of night."

"Sure it does," Adam objected. "As you say, we're public figures, but my brother needs some time to himself once in a while. Using a small airstrip at night reduces the chances of his being seen—" he almost said *getting caught* "—coming and going."

"A lot of NASCAR fans vacation in Mexico. I'm not sure his chances of going unrecognized there would be any better than they are here."

"You go where you're comfortable to relax."

He was full of truisms, but they still didn't quite add up. Why travel more than fifteen hundred miles to go fishing when there was excellent fishing, both salt and freshwater, within an hour or two of Charlotte? Why spend time with an open-wheel driver who's interested in tackling NASCAR instead of inviting him to witness the action itself?

No, those were two good excuses for Trey's mysterious absences, but they weren't satisfactory explanations.

There were, however, two other possibilities that entered her mind.

The first and more appealing one to Tara's romantic nature was that Adam's younger brother was visiting a woman in Old Mexico. No woman had been alluded to in any of the blog entries, but then Roberto Castillo hadn't been mentioned, either. Why the secrecy? Was there something about the woman that the other Sanfords didn't approve of, or that Trey felt his fans might not approve of? Unlike Brent, who, like his father, had developed something of a reputation as a woman-izer—at least he wasn't married—Trey was low-key and discreet in his relationships with women. Was it possible Trey had a family down there that he was keeping out of the public eye?

The realist in Tara conjured up another possible reason for Trey Sanford's clandestine trips to Mexico, one that was far less savory.

"He's been successful so far," Adam said, referring to Trey's ability to stay out of the media spotlight. "Well, up until now. How did you find out about his trips, by the way?"

Ignoring the questions, she declared, "I have another theory about what's going on."

He waited, his gaze wary. "And what might that be?"

"He's buying drugs."

CHAPTER SEVEN

THE SPACE BETWEEN THEM became very still. If Tara had felt uncomfortable with Adam before, the sensation increased tenfold now. The glare he sent her conveyed a distinct desire to see her disappear. She would have done so if she could have. His tone, when it came, however, was remarkably calm and businesslike.

"I hope, Tara—" he spoke like an indulgent father "—you're not accusing my brother of drug trafficking or the illegal use of narcotics."

She started to stammer a denial, then took control of her voice. "I have simply made an observation," she stated in a manner that suggested *she* was the one who had a right to take umbrage. "You have to admit it looks strange for a guy to do all his flying at night, across a foreign border, into a country that is notorious for being a source of illegal substances."

His unblinking eyes never straying from hers, his posture unyielding, Adam asked, "Are things always what they appear?"

"I'm not saying that."

"Then what are you saying?" His tone was patronizing now. "You either believe my brother is involved in smuggling contraband across the U.S. border, in which case you have a legal and moral obligation to inform the authorities, or you are just being provocative by engaging in character assassination."

Her heart was thumping. "The circumstantial evidence," she insisted, "suggests—"

"So you believe he's a smuggler."

"I didn't say that," she shot back.

"No, you implied it." His words had turned sharp, angry, though he still kept his voice down, almost mellow. "You either believe it or you don't. You can't choose both. So which is it?"

He was calling her bluff, and she felt like a fool for even playing his game. She lowered her head and shook it slowly from side to side. "No, I don't think—"

"Good. Be very careful about what you say in print, Tara. Any suggestion that I or either of my brothers is involved in criminal conduct will lead to legal action—against you. I have a moral and ethical obligation to protect my family's reputation and good name, and I will do so strenuously."

What was it with this guy? Whenever she said anything he didn't like or he perceived to be the least bit challenging, he was ready to call out the dogs. Why was he so defensive? Didn't he realize that his menacing attempts at intimidation were just fanning the flames of her suspicion?

"I'm sorry my questions have stirred up so much concern, Adam. I doubt my telling you I'm not the bad guy or that I have no intention of hurting you or your family will do any good at this point. But I do hope you'll give me the benefit of the doubt long enough to cooperate with me on my book. I want to project a positive image of NASCAR and its people."

He gazed at her. She could see he was trying to make up his mind about something. She waited.

"I read your book *Rolling Uphill*," he finally said.

It was the story of a sixteen-year-old boy who'd been a high-school track star until a car accident robbed him of the use of his legs. His goal had been to run the Ascentathon, a notoriously difficult marathon course that started at the base of a mountain and ended at the top, an uphill battle all the way. What took a seasoned Olympic runner four hours to complete took Daniel Wallingford nearly twenty-two hours to complete in his wheelchair, but he got there.

"An inspiring story."

"An inspiring kid," she responded.

They gazed at each other in silence for what seemed like several minutes, though in reality it probably wasn't more than a few seconds.

"Somehow I've rubbed you the wrong way, Adam," she said, "and for that I'm sorry. Clearly you don't trust me. I don't know who in the media betrayed your confidence or how, but I can certainly sympathize. Betrayal leaves us feeling dirty, violated."

He raised a brow, apparently surprised, if not persuaded, by her analysis.

She went on, "Writers don't always get it right. Some have agendas. Some are lazy. Some just don't know any better."

"And you?" he asked, not in a threatening way, but the challenge was unmistakable.

"My only agenda is to write a good, uplifting book about people I find exciting and interesting."

When he didn't respond, she continued, "I'm not lazy. I do my research, but that doesn't always give me the whole story or the complete truth. I'm asking for your input because I want to get it right."

"Why us? Why the Sanford family?"

She could have teased that they were three handsome bachelors, but she sensed he was sincerely seeking an honest answer.

"Because you're interesting. You have scandals in your family and business. Your stories are tales of triumph over adversity that can uplift people who are fighting their own battles in a world that doesn't always draw distinctions between individuals. I promise to be as objective and dispassionate as possible in presenting information. For what it's worth, I also believe in innocent until proved guilty. I don't intend what I write to hurt you, your family or the people who surround you."

With his elbows on the upholstered arms of his chair, he linked his hands in front of his flat abdomen and studied her intently enough to make her self-conscious, if not uncomfortable.

"If you can accept me on that basis, Adam," she concluded, "we can work together. I'd like us to. I'd like to get to know you and the people around you better. If those terms are unacceptable, tell me and I'll leave."

THE BALL WAS in his court. Trust her or kiss her goodbye. He'd definitely like to kiss her—but not goodbye. Yet he still wasn't convinced he could trust her. Brent would advise him not to give her a chance to mess with his life. Trey would say everything in life was a gamble, and his mother would tell him to follow his heart.

But this wasn't a matter of heart. Besides, the last time he'd followed his heart—or was it his hormones—it led him to disaster. He definitely didn't want to go through that again emotionally, and he wasn't sure he could survive it financially.

He stood up. "I promised you a tour of Sanford Racing. Do you still want it?"

She didn't jump at the offer or to her feet. She gazed up at him with a searching quality that stirred something deep inside him.

"Is this just a tour, Adam," she asked, "or are you willing to cooperate with me, give me an in-depth interview and allow me to interview people on your staff and in your family?"

In for a penny… "Yes."

He hoped he wouldn't regret it, but what choice did he have? If he turned her away she wouldn't stop. She'd only pursue information elsewhere and not necessarily from sources who were friendly to Sanford Racing. At least this way he could monitor her access and maybe gain her sympathy when it came to the many conflicts and scandals Sanfords had been involved in over the years.

He wouldn't mind having her around, either. She certainly wasn't hard to look at. He liked the way she occasionally tilted her head to one side and swept her shoulder-length blond hair back with the flick of her hand. He liked the timbre of her voice, too, especially when she laughed. There was an earthiness in the sound, yet also a hint of the kind of softness only a woman possessed.

He was going to be in trouble if he didn't get his mind off her femininity, but how could he look and listen to this creature and not respond?

They returned downstairs to the fabrication shop, the rapport between them somewhat restored, though he kept reminding himself to be on guard—anything he said could and probably would be used against him.

"Are you a NASCAR fan?" He wondered why he hadn't thought to ask the question earlier.

"Want to play trivia? Name the champions from day one?" She smirked. "My folks have a motor home that they've parked on the infield practically every weekend for as long as I can remember. When I was growing up we didn't get to many races that weren't on the East Coast because of the time it took to drive there and the pesky little detail that my sisters and I had to attend school. But even discounting those races, there haven't been too many we've missed over the years."

He was impressed. He also knew following NASCAR that closely wasn't cheap.

"What does your father do for a living?" he asked.

"He's retired now, but he owned—still owns, actually—half a dozen auto repair and body shops, and Mom sells cosmetics through a national distributor. They're not rich, but they're comfortable. Still go to as many races as they can."

Adam felt suddenly like an idiot. First, he hadn't bothered to ask her if she was a NASCAR fan, and now… "Your father does auto repair and body work, and you're letting me explain body fabrication to you."

She chuckled good-naturedly. "You've done a good job of it, too."

"But I haven't told you anything you don't already know," he concluded.

"Well, no. I've got two sisters, no brothers. Dad never had any problem with us girls hanging around the shop, asking questions, sometimes helping out. As long as we didn't get in the way and safety wasn't compromised. So, yeah, I know a little about body construction and auto mechanics."

"You could have said something." But he was more amused now than annoyed.

"I could have," she admitted a bit smugly, "but it was more fun this way. Thanks, by the way, for not talking down to me. I know you thought I had no idea what I was looking at, but you treated me like I was ignorant, not stupid. There's a difference and I appreciate your respecting it."

The praise was unanticipated and it touched him. "If I had thought you were stupid, Tara, I wouldn't have bothered trying to explain it to you in the first place. Now before I make myself redundant again, tell me what you know about engine building."

"Well…" she drawled, "I know what pistons and cylinders and valves and rings are. Cam shafts, timing chains, carburetors—"

"Okay," he said with a satisfied chuckle. "I think I get the picture. I don't have to explain about the big wheels and the little wheels inside an engine block."

They moved into the engine-building shop. Knowing her background now, he wasn't surprised by the questions she posed to him or the engineer who was busy with an engine under construction, but he was impressed by them. He couldn't imagine her pretty little hands grimy with grease and carbon, but at some point he was sure they had been. He admired her for it, but preferred the look of her hands as they were now, long, slender fingers with pearl-pink polish on the nails.

Maybe he hadn't talked down to her before, but now that he knew she was better informed than he'd realized, he was able to be less guarded in the terms he used to discuss both the mechanics and the strategy of racing.

"Would you like to come back tomorrow?" he asked as he escorted her to her bright-yellow car. "I don't know who will be here, since this is our official downtime until after the first of the new year, but you can interview whoever shows up."

"That would be great!"

"Come in around ten, and I'll take you to lunch afterward."

"Oh, I wish I could, but I have other appointments in the morning. I doubt I'll be able to get here before two."

She showed up at one-thirty, dressed in black jeans and a red cowl-neck wool sweater. Her early arrival was fortunate, because she was able to catch a couple of members of the pit crew who'd stopped by on their way to a local sports center where they worked out with personal trainers. One was a jack man, the guy who jumped off the wall carrying the twenty-pound hydraulic jack that was used to hoist the side of the car off the ground so tires could be changed. The other was a tire carrier, who handed off the new tires and took the used ones from the changers. Both jobs required enormous physical strength, and it showed. Since all pit-crew jobs were only for one racing season, both men had to reapply for their jobs again in a couple of months, a good incentive for staying in shape.

"Do you have any plans for this coming weekend?" he asked her when he escorted her to the parking lot this time.

She shook her head. "Not really. Mall flew back to New York this morning. I need to get some writing done."

"I'm driving up to the family compound at Lake Norman tomorrow. I thought you might like to come along to see it and fill out the picture a little more."

"Oh, Adam," she cried. "I'd love to! Will anyone else be there?"

Was she wondering about propriety, a chaperon? He wasn't suggesting an assignation, though he wouldn't mind one.

"My mother and maybe Brent," he told her. "Trey has a full schedule of appearances, so he'll be on the road." He could see the cogs turning in her head: interviews. "I'll pick you up at your place Saturday morning around ten, if that's all right. We have a heated pool, so bring a swimsuit." *A minimal swimsuit, please. I'd like to see more of you.*

TARA WAS NERVOUS Saturday morning as ten o'clock approached. She had a feeling Adam wouldn't be late, as she had been for their first appointment, and she wasn't nearly ready. What should she take with her to Lake Norman? She'd packed her bathing suit, a new one she'd bought just the day before. Unfortunately it hadn't been on sale, even in the middle of December, but she was sure it was worth the price. At least she hoped so.

Adam had chilled out after their initial scraps. He'd become pleasant and relaxed, though she sensed he was still on guard. She hadn't told him that she understood his reference to being raked over the coals by the media. His messy divorce several years ago had been in newspapers, all over the Internet and even the subject of talk shows.

The media's version was that he'd been playing around with his wife's best friend, and that his infidelity had led to the end of his marriage. He'd strenuously denied cheating on his wife, but the divorce judge hadn't seen it that way and saddled him with an unbelievable payout. It had later been reduced, but that didn't change the damage to his reputation.

The question was who Tara believed. His ex-wife and his supposed lover, or Adam?

Tara went back to the Internet to review the coverage about him. Two years ago when the story had been front-page tabloid news, she had been ready to accept, if not actually believe, he was guilty. After all, here was this Hollywood-handsome millionaire, whose father had been a notorious womanizer, yada, yada, yada.

That was before Tara had met him and found he was even more handsome in person than he was in his pictures. But if he was guilty as charged, why did he still bear the media a grudge? Why not just drop the issue and move on?

The mantel clock in the living room was striking the appointed hour when her doorbell rang. Her suitcase lay open at the foot of the bed, clothes spread across the mattress and on her armchair, hanging from the drawers of her dresser, tossed over the corners of the mirror. Would they dress for dinner at his mother's house or would they be casual? For that matter, would there be other guests? The only people he'd mentioned were his mother and brother. She was looking forward to meeting both of them.

The bell rang a second time. *Make up your mind,* she told herself. *Dress up or casual?*

"Coming," she called as she bolted from the bedroom, the issue still unresolved. Pulling the bedroom door closed on the way, she raced across the living room, stopped short, straightened the collar of her pressed yellow blouse, took a deep breath and opened the door.

"Hi. Right on time." She stepped back and invited him in. At least the living room was presentable.

He crossed the threshold. "Ready, or do you need a few more minutes? We're in no hurry."

She hated to tell him she could use another hour. "Just give me a minute to freshen up, and I'll be right with you. Sit down. Make yourself comfortable."

Instead of sitting, however, he wandered over to the sofa table where she had framed pictures of her parents and sisters.

He pointed to a statuesque blonde in a family photo. "Who's that?"

"My younger sister, Emma-Lee. She lives in Atlanta."

"Is she a NASCAR fan, too?"

"My folks would disown her if she weren't. The three of us practically grew up at the track, at least on weekends."

"What does she do?"

"Anything, everything. She's a secretary right now, but that'll change. She's only twenty-five. That's three years younger than me. She's trying to decide now if she wants to be a rock climber, a rock star, anthropologist or a scuba diver. Before that it was a draw between being a veterinarian or a geologist."

Adam laughed. "An independent soul!"

Tara laughed with him. "We're all distinctive. Mallory has the beauty, I have the brains, and Emma-Lee has the personality."

He gave her a sidelong grin. "I wouldn't concede beauty or personality if I were you."

She wasn't quite sure how to react. It was a compliment, and not a grudging one. He didn't have to say it, whether he meant it or not. Her face warmed. In other circumstances the remark might have been an opening...

"Thanks," she said breezily. "I won't be a minute."

She slipped back into her bedroom and remembered to close the door behind her, so he couldn't see the chaos. Forget it, she told herself. His flattery was a throwaway line. Something a man said to a woman to be nice. That was all it was. It didn't mean anything.

She put both the casual tan pantsuit and the sapphire-blue party dress into the valise. Her lingerie was already packed. That left only her cosmetics. She swept them into a big plastic Baggie and sealed it, just in case something popped when she crushed down the suitcase lid.

Upbraiding herself for not packing last night or getting up earlier that morning—it wasn't as if she'd slept much, thinking about spending a weekend with Adam, even if it was with his mother around—she took one more quick survey of the room. She was probably forgetting something.

Lugging the suitcase off the bed, she threw the door open, remembered the bedroom was a shambles, and quickly grabbed the knob and closed the door behind her. "I'm ready."

He came over and relieved her of the piece of luggage. "You pack bricks in this thing?"

She sighed. "I'm never sure what I'll need, so I usually overpack."

He laughed. "All you need is your bikini."

"Well," she drawled, "I did remember my swimsuit." She almost laughed at the disappointment on his face when she used the word swimsuit. "Shall we go?"

He held the passenger door for her, tossed her suitcase in the back seat, and they set off. This was the first time she'd been in a vehicle with him, and she soon realized a race car driver's blood ran in his veins. He didn't speed—or not much—but he did drive aggressively. She settled back in the soft-leather seat and enjoyed the ride. He was supremely confident as he cut in and out of traffic. She felt perfectly safe with him behind the wheel.

The trip to Lake Norman took less than forty-five minutes. They arrived at a gated estate that sloped down to the water, though from the road the shoreline wasn't apparent. Situated at the end of a long, winding driveway that shielded it from curious passersby sat the house. Weathered brick accented with creamy stone door and window frames, it was two-story topped with a gabled roof and a series of dormers.

"It's beautiful, Adam," she said. "Does your whole family live here?"

"Mom has the house. Brent still has his old bedroom on the second floor, expanded now into a suite with a private outside entrance. Trey has another one at the other end of the house on the ground floor. I've taken over the guest house."

"Privilege of the oldest son?"

He chuckled. "Only because I got there first."

She was seeing another side of Adam Sanford, Tara realized, one she liked very much, the proud family man. Had he and his ex-wife considered having children? Had they been unsuccessful in their attempts? Had it been one of the reasons for their breakup?

At Sanford Racing Tara had considered him arrogant, defensive of his brothers. Here at home she saw him as proud and protective.

"Did you grow up here?" she asked.

"Since I was eight. That's when Dad bought the place. Wasn't quite as nice then as it is now. Mom's done wonders with it."

They came to a halt. As they did the front door of the house opened and a woman stepped out. Tara recognized Kath Sanford from her photos. She was rarely seen or taken notice of at races anymore, apparently by her own choice. She was tall and slim with green eyes and carefully groomed brown hair streaked with blond highlights. Tara got out of Adam's SUV and approached her.

"Mrs. Sanford, I'm Tara Dalton. Thank you so much for having me."

"I'm glad you could make it." The reply was polite rather than warm. She turned to her son, who had retrieved the suitcase. "Take that up to the south guest room, then join us in the kitchen."

Adam kissed her on the cheek as he went by. "Be down in a minute."

"I made a fresh pot of coffee," Kath informed Tara. "Adam tells me you're writing a book about NASCAR."

"Yes, ma'am. I'm featuring two families, the Grossos and the Sanfords."

Kath didn't seem overly interested or impressed. Considering that her son Brent had been accused of sabotaging Kent Grosso's car, her lack of enthusiasm shouldn't be surprising. She led Tara through a large, sunny living room to a kitchen that was bigger than Tara's apartment. The outside wall had a row of diamond-shaped windows overlooking a flagstone patio. Beyond it, gossamer wisps of mist rose from a swimming pool. The grounds were meticulously maintained and remarkably colorful, considering it was December.

Kath pointed to a stool for Tara to take on the outer perimeter of a black marble counter, while she went behind it and lifted a carafe from a coffee machine. She filled two large china mugs with the Sanford Racing crest on them.

"Do you take cream and sugar?"

"Yes, please," Tara replied.

Kath moved a sugar bowl over from beside the coffee-maker and retrieved a container of half-and-half from the right side of the huge stainless-steel refrigerator next to it.

"I read *Rolling Uphill.*" She returned the carafe to its

stand. "It was very good." The praise wasn't gushing, but Tara decided it was sincere.

"Thank you." She spooned sugar into her mug. "I hope I'm not abusing your hospitality, Mrs. Sanford, but I would very much like to interview you while I'm here. It won't take too long, maybe an hour, if you're willing."

Kath took a sip of her hot black coffee. "I figured that was why Adam brought you here."

It wasn't the most gracious response, Tara mused, but it was frank. She was beginning to understand where Adam got his cool approach. She heard footsteps behind her, but before she could turn, Adam was pulling out the stool beside her.

"I thought we'd have a late lunch," Kath told her son as she filled another mug and set it before him, "around one, if that's all right. That'll give you time for a swim if you like." She turned to Tara. "We can talk afterward."

"Thank you," Tara said again.

"Is Brent here?" Adam asked.

"He will be for dinner."

CHAPTER EIGHT

THE HOUSE WAS very much as Tara had expected, traditional with distinctively feminine touches in the living room and kitchen, while the den and library were clearly masculine domains. Everything was perfectly maintained and tastefully displayed, with an entire room devoted to trophies and awards, many of them earned by Adam's late father.

"He had quite a record of achievement," Tara said to Adam. "The first driver to take the checkered flag three times in a row after starting off in the last position. The most suspensions in one season. The most DNFs in one season. That was the same year he had the most track wins, yet didn't come close to winning the championship."

"Dad didn't believe in doing things by half."

"It must have been hard on your mother when he died."

She wasn't referring to the way he died, but she could see he thought she was. Wild Bobby earned his name even in death. It had made all the headlines and television news shows, and of course the blogs, that Bobby Sanford had suffered a massive and fatal heart attack while on a romantic weekend with a woman whom he was having an affair with. Perhaps it had been the notorious life he had lived that convinced the media they had the right to exploit the scintillating details of his last hours and minutes, regardless of its effects on the people he'd left behind. Whatever their excuse, Tara understood why Adam and the rest of the family resented the media.

She was about to say so when he said, "Death is always hard, but Mom's a trouper. She does what she has to do."

Tara's recollection was that at the time of her husband's death, Kath Sanford issued a single statement expressing the conventional sentiments appropriate to the loss of a family member while praising his achievements in NASCAR. She had refused to grant interviews, and her three sons followed her example. As a result, the subject of Wild Bobby's death disappeared from the radar almost as quickly as it had popped up.

Missing among the many photographs, Tara noted, were family pictures of Wild Bobby. Nor was there any mention of his death among the many framed news clippings. It was as if the family were ignoring his passing.

Tara fully expected Adam to warn her not to probe too personally. Instead, he said, "You can look at these later. Now let's go swimming."

He escorted her upstairs to a large, sun-filled room with French doors leading onto a small balcony. The room itself was cozy and feminine, held a four-poster with a ruffled canopy, a delicately carved vanity table and a club chair with a hassock next to a small lamp table. The curved shade was white silk and altogether charming.

"I'll meet you poolside in about ten minutes." Adam checked behind the bathroom door. "There's a robe here if you need it."

That was what she'd forgotten!

She unpacked hurriedly, hung her dress in the closet, tossed her other clothes in the chest of drawers and her cosmetic bag in the spacious private bathroom. She changed into her bathing suit, grabbed the thick terry bathrobe from the back of the door and took the stairs at the end of her balcony to the pool below.

He was already there, skimming leaves off the steaming water with a net on a long pole.

The sight of his bare torso made her heart do a little jig. His shoulders were broad, his chest tapering down to a narrow waist and hips. His red paisley bathing suit was trunks-style but not baggy. His legs were long and muscular.

The weather would have been comfortably warm for December—if she had been fully clothed—but it was chilly in just a bathing suit, even with the robe on, yet he seemed totally at ease in the still air wearing less. Not even a goose bump that she could see—and she was definitely looking. She understood why as soon as she drew closer. The water was one source of warmth. Another was the overhead heating coils spaced discreetly along the perimeter of the deck around the pool.

He looked up at her approach. "Come closer." He smiled. "It's warmer here."

And he was hot!

"Water temperature is ninety degrees."

"Sounds perfect." At the foot of a chaise she opened her robe. He'd halted his skimming motions to watch her. His chest did her the great honor of expanding when she dropped the robe on the arm of the chaise. Her heart skipped a beat. She'd selected a midnight-blue one-piece swimsuit that left her back bare.

"Nice suit," he murmured as he unabashedly scanned her from head to foot.

She would have liked to return the compliment by remarking on his intriguing paisley, but didn't dare let her eyes wander in that direction. "Thanks."

She moved to the edge of the pool and stuck her big toe into the water. "Mmm, that is nice and warm." Another kind of heat crept up her legs.

"Shall we take the plunge?" he asked with a smile.

He dove in, leaving barely a ripple on the misty surface of the water. She dropped in feetfirst. The water was glorious.

If Adam thought Tara had been a distraction in the sexy black evening dress she'd worn to the NASCAR banquet, this was even worse...or better. He'd brought her here to meet his mother and brother, hoping it would complete the research she wanted to do. Then, he figured, he could say goodbye to her and move on without any pangs of conscience for his initial bad manners. He certainly wanted to say goodbye to the writer, but did he want to say goodbye to the woman?

She was a strong swimmer, and they both completed a few laps. When she finally ascended the ladder, he found himself preoccupied with the sight of her naked back, the curve of hips and the contours of her long legs, as she dried herself.

"Today is Larine's afternoon off," Kath explained when they returned fully dressed ninety minutes later to the country kitchen. "She made a light lunch for us, though, before she left."

Lunch was hearty potato soup from a black-iron pot, a spinach-and-bean-sprout salad with homemade strawberry-and-poppyseed vinaigrette dressing, and turkey-and-bacon sandwiches on crisp kaiser rolls.

"The iced tea is sweet," Kath told Tara. "I can fix hot if you prefer."

"Sweet tea," Tara said with a smile. "I'm a Southern girl."

They sat at the glass-topped table in the eating nook. Adam enjoyed his food while he listened to his mother conduct her own interview of their guest. He could tell Tara was well aware of what was going on and took it in stride. Dessert was a platter of brownies. He and Tara each took one. His mother took two.

Tara offered to help with the cleanup; Kath let her, not that there was much to do besides put a few dishes in the dishwasher and wipe down the table.

"Now that I've grilled you," Kath said when they were finished, "let's go into the living room so you can interview *me*."

"I'll come along," Adam announced, surprised at his mother's willingness to talk.

TARA HADN'T BEEN expecting Adam to join them and wasn't particularly pleased when he announced he would, but being here on sufferance left little she could do about it. She doubted his presence would make much difference in Kath's responses, anyway.

The living room was large, the outside wall all floor-to-ceiling windows. Because the room had a southern exposure and the towering trees immediately beyond it were bare of leaves at this time of year, the room was flooded with watery winter light. Tara imagined that in the heat of summer, with sunbeams filtered through the leaves of those trees, the room would be shadowy and cool.

A white-marble fireplace with a raised green-marble hearth dominated another wall and was flanked with white bookcases. Their shelves were filled with as many objects as there were books—ginger jars, teapots, silver-framed photos, small pieces of sculpture.

"What do you want to talk about?" Kath asked when they sat on sofas facing each other across a coffee table. Adam was at the other end of his mother's sofa, observing Tara.

"I know the statistics and I've seen the videos of most of the big races," Tara said. "What I'm really interested in is the human side of the racing family. In my research I haven't found much about you, Ms. Sanford. How did you and your husband meet? How did you balance his busy racing career with bringing up a family? What was he like as a father?"

"You're right that not much has been written about me," Kath replied. "The boys can give you a better idea of what Bobby was like as a dad. As for how Bobby and I met…"

Tara sat forward with interest.

"We went to the same high school, but we actually met at

a race track, a dirt track south of Concord. It isn't there anymore. He was driving a Studebaker. I was driving a Hudson."

"Whoa!" Tara exclaimed. "You were a driver? I didn't know that."

Kath laughed, clearly enjoying the moment. "Not for very long. I loved the speed, even though it scared me—maybe *because* it did. I beat him that day. We were neck and neck all the way. On the next-to-last lap I got up my nerve and started forcing him to the left. He could either get crumpled— I knew how much he loved that jalopy of his—fall behind me or violate the inside line and be disqualified."

"What did he do?" Tara asked.

Kath snickered. "Took his foot off the gas and let me pull ahead of him. He figured he'd overtake me on the next lap, but he never did—" she smiled complacently "—and I won the race."

Adam chuckled, obviously enjoying Tara's surprise at this little-known side of his mother.

"I don't imagine Bobby was very happy about that," Tara noted.

This time Kath let out a rare, full-throated guffaw. "Mad as a wet hen, I can tell you. Stomped up and down in front of me afterward, calling me all sorts of things."

"What did you do?"

"What my own mother used to do when my father was making a fool of himself. Waited till he was finished, then told him to get over it. He'd been outraced. Tough."

Tara snickered. "And then?"

"We raced against each other three more times. I won two of them, then blew my engine in the third. Couldn't afford to build another car, and my folks weren't willing to help. They'd tolerated my racing, but had never been enthusiastic about it. They felt it wasn't appropriate for a young lady."

Kath's expression softened. "The surprise was Bobby's reaction. When he found out I wouldn't be building another car, he came to see me, said he was real sorry I was quitting, because he thought I was a good driver and he enjoyed racing against me. I was stunned. From the way he'd treated me at the track and ignored me at school, I figured he couldn't stand me. I knew he took a lot of heat from his friends about being beat by a *girl*. Then he completely shocked me by asking me to join his team as a mechanic."

"You were a gearhead?" Tara was astonished.

Adam grinned at her.

His mother awarded her a self-satisfied smile. "Let me tell you I could tear down and rebuild a carburetor faster than Bobby could any day."

"As I recall he just happened to be pretty good," her son contributed.

"He was damn good," Kath agreed. "I was better."

Tara shook her head and laughed. "Why did you stop racing, Ms. Sanford?"

"We got married. I got pregnant with Adam, then a year later with Brent."

"So you had to choose," Tara said. "Ever have any regrets?"

Kath looked over at her son. "Racing was fun. I enjoyed it and did it well, but being a mother was more fulfilling. Besides, I'm not sure I could have made it beyond the dirt track."

"Didn't you ever want to find out?" Tara asked.

"Of course I did, but things in life don't always work out the way we want or expect them to. We do what we must the best we know how."

There was subtext here, Tara realized, and wondered if she should pursue it. Had Adam not been sitting across from her, if it had been just Kath and her, she might have, but not with him watching her. What the two women had had in common, even more than a love of NASCAR and an unconventional mechanical ability, was philandering husbands. Tara had divorced the creep she'd been married to. Kath had stuck by her man. Because she still loved him and hoped one day to reform him? Because of the children? Tara had never had any, another strike against her marriage. When Tara had decided to call it quits with Spenser, she'd also discovered she no longer loved him. Did that mean she never had? Had she been attracted to him for the wrong reasons? It would have been fascinating and no doubt instructive to discuss such matters with Kath, this older woman who'd experienced so much.

Adam's presence prevented it now, but of course that had been his intent all along, to keep her from asking his mother potentially hurtful or embarrassing questions. Tara should resent him and his distrust of her discretion, and maybe a part of her did, but she also had to admire the protective knight in him. Her dad was like that; Spenser certainly hadn't been.

"I remember the first time I saw that picture of you in the family album," Adam told his mother, "wearing a driving helmet. I automatically assumed it was Dad's, and that you were just having fun putting it on."

Again Kath smiled at him, but it seemed to Tara there was a secret satisfaction in it, as if she was remembering a happier time in her life. Maybe giving up racing hadn't been quite as easy as she made it out to be.

The three of them sat and talked for another hour, but nothing came out of it that was as earth-shattering as Kath's former role as a dirt-track driver and engine specialist.

They were about to break up when Adam's brother strode into the room.

Brent wasn't quite as tall as Adam, but he had the unmistakable Sanford presence. Rather than take after his mother in looks, he more closely resembled the photographs of Wild Bobby Tara had seen.

He leaned over and kissed his mother on the cheek before letting Adam introduce Tara. Like his father, he'd had a reputation as a ladies' man, the only redeeming factor being that he wasn't married. According to various blogs, that propensity hadn't changed since he'd left the track.

When he took Tara's hand to shake, she half expected him to raise her fingers to his lips and kiss them. Oh, she decided, he definitely had charm, but a woman would be a fool to fall under its power. She also saw the wariness come to his playful dark eyes when Adam identified her as a writer.

"I'm going to get dinner started," Kath announced, rising. "Are we going to have cocktails tonight in honor of our guest?"

"If not in her honor," Brent said, "how about because we want them."

"I'll have my usual Manhattan," Kath announced, and went toward the kitchen.

"I'm a vodka-martini man," Brent informed Tara as he went over to a wet bar in the corner. "Adam favors gin-and-tonic. What can I get you?"

"A gin-and-tonic sounds refreshing." She tried to remember the last time she'd drunk gin.

"Mom just told Tara about her dirt-track racing days," Adam informed his brother.

Brent stopped pouring the bourbon for his mother's cocktail. "So the secret will be out, huh? I can see the head-lines now. *His mother was a gearhead!*" He chuckled and finished the drink preparation and handed a frosty highball glass to their guest, then his brother.

"You better watch this woman," he advised Adam. "She could be very dangerous."

CHAPTER NINE

"Do you miss racing?" Tara asked.

She and Brent were sitting in the library. Dinner wouldn't be for another hour. To her amazement he'd agreed to give her a private interview when she asked him over cocktails. Perhaps his mother and brother having already spoken to her *on the record* influenced his decision. Whatever the reason, she was sure the decision had been solely his. This time Adam hadn't suggested he sit in on the discussion. To Tara's immense relief. Not only would his presence have inhibited spontaneous communications between her and Brent, as it had between her and Kath, but his close proximity made her nervous. It wasn't just the memory of him in his swimsuit, his body slick, his hair wet and shiny, it was the man himself. She was loath to admit it, but it was almost as if she kept seeking his approval, those little nods that indicated his agreement with what she was asking.

"I thoroughly enjoy what I do," Brent responded. He'd brought his drink with him and now took a sip.

Tara had a choice, let him get away with the non-answer and come away from the session with pabulum, or call him on it and take the chance of alienating him.

"I'm glad," she said, "but that doesn't answer my question. I never see you at races. Don't you miss NASCAR, the roar and excitement of it?"

He studied her with his dark, impenetrable eyes. He was

at a crossroads, too. "I drove in the NASCAR Camping World Truck Series, Tara, in the NASCAR Nationwide and the NASCAR Sprint Cup Series for fifteen years. Of course I miss it." There was an edge in his voice, though she could tell he was trying very hard to dull it. Like all great athletes, he was a man of self-discipline. One couldn't succeed in a competitive endeavor without controlling one's emotions, and until he quit racing, Brent had been very successful, having won a long string of races. He'd been a top contender for the NASCAR Sprint Series Cup championship when an accusation had destroyed his career.

"You know I have to ask about the scandal and your quitting, Brent," she said sympathetically.

Until the awards dinner she'd been inclined to believe he was guilty as charged. The evidence against him had appeared incontrovertible; the fact that he had walked away rather than put up a fight only seemed to confirm that the allegations against him were true. Alan Cargill had changed all that with a few words Friday night, but what was behind the words?

"I've read all the stories that have been published," she continued, "and a lot of the speculation floating around cyberspace. Most of it is pretty damning. I'd like to hear your side of the story."

"That's refreshing." He studied her for a moment. He didn't apologize for the sarcasm, but his demeanor said he regretted it. Crunch time. Steepling his long fingers contemplatively, he said, "I wish I could make sense of it. Let me start with the sequence of events."

She nodded.

"Just before the second Talladega race of the season four years ago, Adam brought Alan Cargill to see me. Kent Grosso was driving for Cargill Motors at the time—before switching to Maximus Motorsports—and had just been disqualified from the race because his fuel was contaminated. I was stunned. Everybody's heard about how old Milo Grosso had been cheated out of a championship years before because Connor Murphy had messed with his fuel. If a Grosso wanted to cheat, it seemed to me fuel contamination would have been the last way any of them would have chosen.

"Cargill stated they'd been sabotaged by their gas man, Mike Jones. My immediate question was why are you coming to me about any of this? Cargill explained that Jones had begun to suffer pangs of conscience, came to him and confessed that I had bribed him to do it."

Brent's chest expanded as he heaved a great sigh. "I told him the accusation was absolutely outrageous. I looked to my brother. Was he asking me to sit out this race? Adam promised his full and unqualified support. The decision was mine. I'd taken the pole for that race. I was certain I was headed for Victory Lane. But Cargill had pulled the rug out from under me. I was furious. My concentration was shot. I raced and finished dead last. Needless to say I didn't react well afterwards."

"According to some reports," Tara noted, "you threatened Cargill."

Brent shook his head. "That isn't true. I did say some things I later regretted. My emotions were running high, but I never threatened him. I was just mad as hell. Under the circumstances I think I had a right to be."

"Go on," she urged, when he seemed inclined to lapse into silence.

She had no doubt he'd relived this series of events hundreds of times, and that even after four years, recounting it was still painful. She also knew the media hadn't been gentle or sympathetic toward him. She was a little surprised, therefore, given Adam's undisguised animosity toward journalists, that Brent had agreed to talk to her at all. He'd turned down numerous requests—and reputedly offers of big bucks—to discuss it with various members of the media in the past few years.

"I demanded proof of the allegations," he continued. "According to Jones, a member of the Sanford Racing team had called him and asked him to meet me at the Speedway Bar. You probably know it. It's been a popular place with race people for years. I'd been there more than once myself. I insisted I didn't know this guy, Jones, and had never met him. The investigators produced surveillance tapes from the bar that showed us together."

"Were the tapes doctored in any way?" Tara asked. The video was available on the Internet. She'd viewed it several times. It appeared seamless and authentic, and technical experts had insisted that it was.

"It's for real," Brent replied. "I remembered the encounter after I'd seen it. One of those chance meetings. Two guys come up to the bar. They say a couple of words to each other casually, get their drinks and split. Except that it was obvious from the tapes that Jones was acting suspiciously, constantly looking over his shoulder as if he was paranoid. I was standing next to him, not paying any attention. There wasn't a mirror behind the back bar for me to observe him. A minute after I walked away he moved off camera in the same direction."

"No audio?"

"In a bar?" Brent snorted. "Everybody knew there were surveillance cameras for security, but if anyone ever suspected their conversations were being listened to or recorded, the place would have cleared out in a NASCAR minute. You may have to watch what you do in public places, but speech is still free."

"Tell me about the money," Tara prompted.

He glared at her for a second, then retreated. "Up to this point it was still my word against Jones's. Our verbal exchange had been very brief. There was no way to determine what was said. The angle of the shot was such that our lips couldn't be read. According to Jones, however, when we went off camera we struck up a deal. I supposedly gave him five hundred bucks in cash and a promise for ten grand if he would contaminate Kent Grosso's fuel on Sunday. The evidence he offered was his deposit slip into his checking account the next morning for exactly five hundred dollars."

"Why would Jones set *you* up, Brent? I mean, why you *personally?* Why not someone else?"

Brent's jaw tightened and his concentration seemed to turn inward for several seconds before he exhaled in obvious frustration.

"Good question," he finally acknowledged, "and why would a guy confess to sabotaging his own team if it wasn't true? You can ask him those things when I find him. All I know is that I was instantly put on the defensive. The video mysteriously found its way onto the Internet, and the press had a field day. My denials all sounded hollow in light of that video after I'd publicly denied ever meeting Jones. The deposit slip…in itself it wasn't conclusive proof of anything, either, but then Jones disappeared, vanished. One reporter even had the b— the audacity to suggest I killed him to shut him up. Jones had admitted to taking a bribe and sabotaging his own team. Now all of a sudden, he was being portrayed as the victim. It didn't make sense, especially since his disappearance left me helpless, damned for something I hadn't done by someone I couldn't question or argue with."

"So you walked away." Tara saw his frown of pain and added, "It couldn't have been easy."

He stared momentarily at the ceiling. "It was hell. Adam and my mother wanted me to fight it out with NASCAR, in the press and in court, if necessary, and I seriously considered it, believe me. The problem was I always seemed to come across as making excuses, giving alibis, denying things, instead of being able to affirm them. NASCAR suspended me from racing after their investigation. How could they not? The evidence was stacked against me. So the season was lost for me, in spite of the fact that I had been ahead in wins and points going into Talladega. I had a right to appeal their decision, but without new evidence, without being able to confront Mike Jones and call him a liar, I knew I didn't have a chance."

"What about Trey?" Tara asked.

"What about him?"

"You said Adam and your mother urged you to fight. Didn't Trey?"

"The whole family was behind me." He sat motionless, his hands resting on the arms of the chair, but his frustration was palpable. "A legal battle would have gone on for months, maybe years, and in the end I would have been just as tainted as I was when I started. My only hope was and is for me to find Mike Jones and convince him to recant his charge against me."

"Any luck so far?"

He shrugged his wide shoulders. "Obviously not. Believe me, I've looked. Hard. I've followed leads in a host of places, but so far I haven't been able to find a trace of him."

"If…when you get this resolved, will you race again?"

She saw infinite sadness in his attempt at nonchalance. "I've moved on, Tara. I like what I'm doing and I'm doing well at it. I'm also getting too old to just slip back into a sport I haven't participated in for four years. All I want now is to be able to go to races without people pointing at my back and whispering that I'm a cheat."

"Thank you for your candor, Brent," Tara said a few minutes later as they climbed to their feet. "Is there anything in what you've told me that you do not want repeated?"

He looked at her in surprise, clearly not expecting the question, then he shook his head. "Everything I've told you is true. You can do whatever you want with it."

DINNER WAS a simple affair—steaks broiled outside on a big stainless-steel grill with Adam officiating, baked potatoes and steamed broccoli. There were just the four of them— Kath, her two sons and Tara. They talked about NASCAR mostly. Tara asked Kath more about her experience as a driver and mechanic. Tara wasn't at all surprised that she was so knowledgeable about every aspect of stock car racing. Most wives and families associated with the sport were immersed in it.

Kath was the first to excuse herself later that evening and retire to her room. Brent hung around a while longer, telling Tara about some of the places his air-charter service had taken him. She had already researched to see if he'd made any dead-of-the-night trips to remote parts of Mexico, but her check of FAA flight plans accounted for all his aircraft's movements, which were consistently north of the border. A few flights went to Canada and Alaska, but she found nothing suspicious, only well-documented charter trips by respected clients.

After Brent went to his quarters, Tara wondered if Adam might suggest another swim. The idea was definitely appealing; however, he didn't.

She should have been exhausted by the day's activities, but she wasn't. In her room she booted up her laptop and transcribed her recordings of the day's two interviews. Still restless an hour later, she opened one of the French doors and stepped out onto the balcony. The night air was cold but still, the lights around the pool were turned off, but she could hear the subtle splash of water. It took a moment for her eyes to adjust to the darkness. Adam was swimming.

Swimming by yourself is not a safe practice, she silently admonished him. She had an obligation to join him—for his own protection—not that she believed he was in serious danger. He was a strong swimmer. The pool was large but not overwhelming.

Was he skinny-dipping? Not likely with his mother at home and his brother not far away. Is that why he hadn't invited her to join him? Because they were nearby?

She stood in the frosty darkness, listening to the steady rhythm of his freestyle strokes, visualizing rather than seeing the flex and release of his well-toned muscles as he burned off excess energy.

She was about to turn, slip back inside and change into her new swimsuit when the sound stopped. She strained to refocus on the man pulling himself out of the water. She couldn't be sure he was wearing the same bathing suit he'd worn earlier that day, but he was definitely wearing something. She watched him pick up a bath sheet from a nearby table—he had to be cold since none of the heating lamps were turned on—wrap himself in it and trudge off in the direction of the guest house.

"Good night, Adam," she whispered and returned to her bedroom.

She crawled under the covers of the four-poster bed thinking about him. Something was changing between them, an indefinable affinity was developing; she couldn't explain why. Their relationship had started as a forced congeniality, based at least partly on physical attraction. It had grown to rapport during their days together at the garage, and now, in the presence of family, was maturing into solicitude, a genuine caring. Where it would lead, she wasn't sure. Whether she should allow it to go anywhere was equally uncertain. What she did know was that she was willing, even eager to participate in the adventure.

When she awoke the next morning the room was already bathed with light. She'd slept much later than she normally did, and she'd dreamed. She couldn't remember exactly what,

·except that Adam had been in it, and it left her with a warm, contented feeling.

Breakfast, when she finally made it downstairs, was clearly an impromptu meal. Brent had a charter flight scheduled for that morning. He'd already eaten and left. Adam was on his second cup of coffee, and Kath had gone to church and was expected back within minutes.

"I hope you like scrambled eggs, because I have half a dozen already beaten."

"You like to cook?" She helped herself to coffee.

"There are a few things I do well. Like breaking eggs. The rest I leave to other people."

"Your mother," she concluded.

"The housekeeper and restaurant chefs," he corrected her. "Don't tell her I said this, but Mom isn't all that great a cook."

"I heard that." Kath marched into the family kitchen. "He's wrong. I'm totally awesome with frozen dinners and packaged brownies."

Tara chuckled. Kath had loosened up with her, as well. She'd been aloof, bordering on formal, when they'd first met yesterday morning. Now she was making self-deprecating jokes.

Adam went over to his mother and kissed her fondly on the cheek. Tara liked his easy demonstration of affection.

"I'll take you up on the eggs," Kath told him.

He turned to Tara. "You're not going to let Mom eat by herself, are you?"

"What about you?"

"I hate eggs." At her shocked expression, he laughed. "Yeah, I'll eat them, too."

They spent a leisurely morning reading the Sunday papers, drinking coffee, but mostly in companionable silence, and to Tara's amazement, it felt absolutely right. There was very little quiet when she was with her parents. Her mother was a chatterbox, and her father always had an opinion. There was no hostility, no animosity, even on the rare occasions when they openly disagreed, just constant babble.

Tara and Adam went for another swim, this one more relaxed, less demonstrative, though hardly less aware. Afterward they spent time in the trophy room. Tara took notes of races and events she wanted to look into in more detail on the Internet when she got home.

Kath gave her a friendly kiss on the cheek when they said goodbye later that afternoon. "I hope you'll come again," she told her guest.

"Thank you for a very enjoyable weekend," Adam said to Tara a minute or two after they'd turned onto the main road headed for Charlotte.

"It's I who should be thanking you, Adam," she returned. "You have a wonderful family. I enjoyed spending time with them. The only one I haven't met is Trey."

A full minute went by. "I want to thank you for not asking Mom the question reporters always seem to wallow in—how did it feel when you learned how your husband had died?"

He still saw her as part of "the media", despite her insistence that she was not a reporter or a journalist in the traditional sense. Under other circumstances, being lumped in with them wouldn't be offensive, but knowing his reason for his animus against them, she was irritated to the point of insult. Had he not been listening?

"There are some emotions that are universal," she said quietly. "No woman has to ask what infidelity feels like."

He cast her a perplexed glance, clearly expecting her to elaborate. When she didn't, he said, "Enough of them did."

"Because they were lazy and insensitive, not because they cared what she felt. I'm not sure anyone who can ask such a question is capable of caring, and I resent being included with them."

"That's my point, Tara. You're different."

It was clarification without an apology. She was tempted to press the issue further, but just then he pulled up in front of her apartment building. He removed her heavy valise from the back seat. When she reached to take it from him, however, he offered to carry it for her.

At her door, she invited him in.

"I'd better not." He put the suitcase down on the floor, then grabbed her around the waist, pulled her close and kissed her solidly on the lips.

She didn't resist. Just as she was beginning to participate, he broke off and gazed at her for a moment.

"Good night, Tara." He turned and fled down the stairs.

She listened to his SUV pull away, unconsciously touching her fingers to her lips. A peck on the cheek would have been an appropriate gesture at the end of a pleasant two-day visit, but the lip lock he'd put on her and the way she'd responded were in no way platonic.

Her lips still tingled and her face felt warm while she unpacked her suitcase. She grinned as she removed her dress and carried it back to the closet. She'd never gotten to wear it, but she had worn her new swimsuit. She remembered how she'd felt as his eyes had roved over her.

The kiss lingered in her mind. She knew where it would lead. The prospect excited her and scared her at the same time. It wasn't as if she hadn't been down this path before— or one uncomfortably like it.

In her kitchen, as she fixed herself a cup of tea, she thought how she'd been attracted to Adam the moment she'd seen him at the NASCAR Awards Banquet. It wasn't solely his looks, though they were mesmerizing. It certainly hadn't been his haughty attitude when they'd finally met. Despite it, there had been something in his green eyes that had drawn her in, enveloped her in a sense of both intrigue and vulnerability.

There'd been a hint of loneliness in them, too, and it resonated with her.

With Spenser Rawls, that air of "I need you, please help me" had been a trap, one she hadn't known she was getting into until it was too late. She hadn't realized he was such a consummate actor.

Her mother had been thrilled when she and Spenser announced their engagement. Her father had been pleased, too. Not only was Spenser Rawls charming and boyishly handsome, he was also filthy rich.

What Tara had missed was that Spenser Rawls had become a force to be reckoned with in the world of corporate law by being cunning and manipulative, talents she belatedly discovered he wasn't able or willing to switch off at the door to hearth and home. Or in the bedroom, for that matter. Secrets might be intriguing and exciting in books and movies. In real life they sowed discontent. He'd kept a lot from her. Most personally devastating, the women he kept, not only for his own diversion and personal entertainment, but for his clients. He even invited some of the women to the same social events he took Tara to. It was his way of laughing at her.

One of the things she'd expected when she married him was that his financial status would allow her the freedom to pursue her own interests and passions, such as writing. Within a couple of months, however, she realized her husband demanded all her time.

Her entreaties for a bit of independence had fallen on deaf ears. She'd been willing to stick the marriage out, try to reform him—until she found out about his chronic infidelities. A year almost to the day after their wedding, she walked out and filed for divorce. She came away with nothing, in some ways with less than nothing, since he'd robbed her of her pride and dignity—until she realized no one had the power to take those away from her; they could only be sacrificed.

She touched her lips again. Adam's kiss had set off alarms, but it had stirred desires, needs, too. Adam was a passionate man. He was also manipulative, a man holding out on her. The question now was how she was going to deal with those issues, with him.

She was falling for another rich man with secrets. Maybe she hadn't learned anything, after all.

CHAPTER TEN

TWO WEEKS WENT BY during which Tara heard and saw nothing of Adam. It gave her uninterrupted time for writing, except she kept gazing off into the distance, thinking about him. What would have happened if she'd joined him in the pool that night? Why did he decline her invitation to come into her apartment when he brought her home that Sunday evening? She knew he was interested in her. His kiss proved that. Was it possible he was as *afraid* as she was of starting a relationship?

Mallory came down to Charlotte for another few days of shooting for *Racing Hearts,* their last episodes before the end of the calendar year, and Tara went back with her to New York to do last-minute Christmas shopping. The trip was not an impediment to Adam calling her, Tara reminded herself, since she always had her cell phone with her, and he knew the number.

She could call him, of course, but on what pretext? That he'd kissed her goodbye and she hadn't gotten a chance to kiss him back?

She'd made a nuisance of herself about the interviews when they first met, and she'd gotten what she wanted. Wasn't the rest up to him? After all, she reminded herself for the millionth time, he'd kissed her.

She needed to stop obsessing over that one little, impulsive kiss, but…

Tara had just returned to Charlotte when she received a

phone call from her parents, a conference call with Mallory in New York and Emma-Lee in Atlanta.

"Would you girls mind if we delayed our return to Charlotte by a few days?" their father, Buddy, asked. "It'll mean celebrating Christmas after the twenty-fifth."

Their mother, Shirley, explained. They had taken a Caribbean cruise with the expectation of getting home in time for the holiday. "But our ship ran into engine trouble, and the captain was forced to pull into a port that wasn't originally on our itinerary for repairs."

"As compensation for the delay," Buddy elaborated, "the cruise line has offered us a choice of air service back home or a side trip to Mazatlán from here once we get under way, all expenses paid."

"You know we've always wanted to go there," Shirley said. "Would you girls be too upset if we took advantage of the free offer?"

"Go for it," Emma-Lee said brightly.

"I agree," Tara chimed in, though she was disappointed. Christmas was a special occasion and they'd always spent it together. Celebrating the holiday on a different day wouldn't be the same, but then, it wasn't as if they were little kids anymore.

"When will you be getting back, then? And where?" Mallory asked.

"The twenty-seventh," Shirley replied.

"The cruise company will pay for airline tickets to wherever we want to go," Buddy said. "We can meet you in Charlotte, in Atlanta or New York."

"We've never done Christmas in New York," Shirley pointed out. "That might be fun."

"New York," Mallory voted before the others had a chance. "I have friends who are going away for the week between Christmas and New Year's. I'm sure I can get them to lend us the use of their apartment for a few days. It's on the upper East

Side, not far from Central Park and the Metropolitan Museum."

"Fantastic," Emma-Lee chimed in. "Let's go for it."

Tara agreed. A couple of days' delay in celebrating the holiday seemed like a small price to pay for the opportunities presented.

After their parents hung up and Emma-Lee signed off, Mallory confessed to Tara that the change in plans actually worked in her favor. The director of *Racing Hearts* gave a spectacular party at his penthouse home every year on Christmas Eve. She offered to see if Tara could be invited, if she wanted to come up to the city early.

Tara was tempted. She loved visiting the Big Apple, and with all the holiday lights up, it would be a sparkling wonderland. But she also had a lot of work to do at home, not just on her book, which was already falling behind her projected schedule, but also on several other writing projects she had been neglecting. So she declined.

Two days before Christmas, feeling low about the approaching holiday, Tara decided to hang the wreath she'd impulsively purchased the day before over her small, prefabricated fireplace. She had just opened the box when her cell phone jingled.

"I just wanted to call and wish you a Merry Christmas," Adam said without saying hello or identifying himself. Not that he needed to. She recognized his voice instantly.

"Same to you and your mother. And your brothers," she added.

"Are your folks coming here, or are you going to meet them somewhere?"

"We're all getting together in New York after Christmas."

"After?"

She explained about their change of plans.

"So what about Christmas Day itself?" He sounded concerned.

"I'm staying here. I'll fly up to New York on the twenty-seventh."

"So that means you're free on Christmas Day." *Free* certainly sounded better than being all alone. "How about spending the day at Lake Norman with me, Mom and my brothers?"

Seeing him again, being with him was appealing, but she hesitated. "I don't know, Adam. It seems like a terrible imposition. Christmas is a family day."

"And you're all alone. So join *our* family."

"Your mother won't mind?"

"Mom will be all for it. She doesn't take to people quickly, but she's taken to you. Please join us. Tomorrow is Christmas Eve. I can pick you up around three and bring you home the morning after Christmas. That ought to give you plenty of time to pack for New York."

"Are you sure? I don't want to get in the way."

He laughed. "You won't. Mom will enjoy having a woman around."

And you? she almost asked. "It's very kind of you."

"Good. It's settled then. I'll be by around three. We tend to graze on Christmas Eve, a lot of nibbling, to leave plenty of room for dinner the next day."

"Sounds like fun. Thank you. I'm looking forward to it."

She disconnected and stared at the phone. Serendipity. It was a wonderful thing. It also meant she would have to scramble for some presents to take with her.

He was punctual the next day, as she knew he would be. This time she was ready and didn't keep him waiting. She'd packed a new red dress and was determined she was going to wear it on Christmas Day.

The greeting she received from Kath was a lot warmer than on the first visit. Brent, too, gave her a welcoming peck on the cheek. Trey wouldn't be joining them until the following

day. Tara was still eager to talk to him about his trips to
Mexico. All of her attempts so far had failed, but she also
reminded herself that this was a family holiday, not an appropriate time to be cross-examining people about their life-
styles. Setting up an appointment wouldn't be impolite,
though, would it?

The Christmas tree, a huge fir, was positioned in front of
the windows in the living room. The decorations were incomplete, however, and Tara was invited to help add the remaining ornaments.

The smells emanating through the kitchen were mouthwa-
tering. Tara soon realized, however, that Kath had nothing to
do with them. Larine, their housekeeper, was the culinary
magician. As Adam had promised, they spent the evening
grazing as Larine brought out platter after platter of treats
ranging from miniature crab cakes to marzipan reindeer with
little red noses. There was wine, eggnog, spiced teas and rich
coffee to drink. Tara didn't eat a lot of anything but sampled
everything, and finally went to bed sometime after midnight,
nutritionally sated and sleepy. To her disappointment, Adam
didn't kiss her good-night before he left for the guest house.

Any notion Tara might have had about getting time alone
with Trey the next day before dinner quickly faded. She was
finishing her last breakfast crepe around ten o'clock when he
arrived with a girlfriend, a statuesque brunette by the name of
Paige who clung to him and his every word during the rekin-
dled breakfast and the family exchange of gifts that followed.
No grandiose presents were given—no new car or boat or
airplane. But Kath received elegant but not ostentatious
jewelry from her sons—diamonds, rubies and pearls—
probably worth a year's earnings for Tara. Adam gave Tara a
massive musical download for her MP3 player, and Kath presented her with a set of silver-ring bracelets. In exchange,
Tara gave Adam a gold pen—what else would a writer give?—

and Kath a figurine she found in an antique shop. Whether it had any value or was even an antique, Tara had no idea, but it was pretty.

The way Paige kept hogging Trey's company, Tara realized she couldn't approach him about an interview without calling attention to herself, and she didn't want to take a chance of alienating Adam by reminding him of her mission. An interview with Trey could wait. Two hours after dinner he and his girlfriend departed.

That night, after Kath and Brent had retired, Adam settled with Tara on one of the couches in the living room. The only light was from the Christmas tree and the logs crackling in the fireplace. He put his arm around her, held her and after a minute lifted up her head and kissed her on the lips, a slow, intense exploration she participated in greedily.

"I thought you might like to see the guest house tonight," he murmured.

The idea was more than intriguing, but not when they were virtually under the eye of his mother.

"Oh, Adam, I don't think that would be a good idea," she confessed. "Not here…tonight—"

He held her chin gently with his fingers and kissed her again. "You're driving me crazy. I hope you know that."

No crazier than he was driving her.

The next morning he drove her home to Charlotte. She invited him into her apartment, and he was about to say yes when Tara's neighbor, Mrs. Olianski, opened her door and rushed over with a platter of cake and cookies that her son had given her the day before. It was clear the sweet old lady had no intention of leaving until she had told Tara all about the previous day's events, about what her grandchildren had given her, about the meal her daughter-in-law had prepared. Considering that Mrs. Olianski spent most of the other 364 days of the year alone in her apartment, Tara didn't have the heart to ask her to leave.

Adam's glance told her he sensed what the situation was, smiled sympathetically and left after accepting a cookie from the aging widow.

IN MID-JANUARY he called to invite Tara to join him at Halesboro. They were planning to put Trey's No. 483 through its paces in preparation for the upcoming season.

"Actually," she said, "I was already planning to meet my parents there. They'll be thrilled to meet you."

The slight hesitation in his reply told her she'd caught him by surprise. Good, she thought. It was about time.

"And I'm looking forward to meeting them," he said. "Where will you be staying?"

"With them in their motor home. My sisters can't make it. Mallory has to stay in New York for some promotion shots *Racing Hearts* has scheduled, and Emma-Lee can't get away from her job in Atlanta. So I'll have the pull-out couch all to myself. Pure luxury."

"I'm taking my motor home, as well," he remarked. "I'll give you a tour of it."

Had he been planning to invite her to stay with him? Would she have accepted? It was an interesting question to speculate about. She was almost glad she didn't have to decide.

"Mom will be thrilled."

CHAPTER ELEVEN

HALESBORO, ABOUT a two-hour drive west of Charlotte, had fallen on hard times. Once thriving, the track itself was still in good condition, but the facilities supporting it had suffered in the past few years, and the town, which depended on the tourist trade the track brought, had likewise declined as fans stopped coming to what was no longer an authorized short track.

Appearances notwithstanding, no two NASCAR tracks were the same. Halesboro fit the standard oval pattern, but turns One and Two were banked at twenty-one degrees, and turns Three and Four were a steep thirty-six. The backstretch was seven. Altogether they made the mile-and-a-half track very fast.

Adam pulled into the infield parking area, which was a maze of weeds and potholes. His motor home was lined up on the far side of the lot with several others. He recognized those belonging to the Grossos, Dean's and Kent's. Adam was a little surprised to see Milo's there, as well. The old-timer and his wife, Juliana, attended few official races anymore, and rarely bothered with test runs. Maybe showing up today was their way of demonstrating support for the new Cargill-Grosso Racing team. Adam imagined the nonagenarian was mighty proud of his family's new ownership status.

Several other motor homes were also parked nearby. Fans and observers, probably. He wondered which one of them belonged to Tara's parents.

He pulled his SUV up not far from his motor home and got out. Immediately the door of a flame-red RV flew open and Tara emerged. The sight of her made his pulse quicken. She was all smiles as she approached. In spite of her quilted jacket, his fantasies were actively focused on her feminine curves. He almost missed the two people following her. When he made a conscious effort to look at the man and woman, he immediately recognized them from the photos he'd seen in her apartment.

The introductions confirmed it.

Tara's father, Buddy, was about six feet tall, large-boned and well fed, with gray hair, blue eyes and a ruddy complexion. Tara had mentioned that he'd played football in high school and that he was essentially a self-made man, having expanded an auto-repair shop into a thriving chain. Adam could easily picture this hulk of a man blocking and tackling forty-plus years earlier. The successful businessman image was a bit more of a challenge.

"Your dad was one of the best drivers I ever saw." Buddy yanked Adam's hand like a jack pump. "I loved watching that man race. He didn't always win, and nobody ever accused him of being a graceful loser, but he made things exciting. You never knew what was going to happen next when Wild Bobby was on the track."

"Brent was a better driver," Tara's mother, Shirley, countered. "More skillful, more subtle and a good sport, win or lose." Was that her way of saying she didn't believe the allegations against him? Had Tara put her mother up to it? "Your dad was good," the older woman went on. "I'm not saying he wasn't, but compared with Brent, he was a bull in a china shop, no disrespect intended."

Adam laughed. "You're not getting any argument from me."

Shirley Dalton had beautiful sandy-colored hair, was only a couple of inches shorter than her husband and quite shapely, in a robust sort of way. Her makeup seemed a tad overdone but not excessive. Tara said she'd been a cheerleader back in high school. Adam imagined she could still execute the routines she'd done for Buddy and his team back when.

"Trey now," she continued, "he may be the best of them."

"Aggressive and smart," Buddy contributed. "A combination you can't beat. He's up against some tough competition this year, though—"

"Mom, Dad, Adam needs to check in with his team," Tara interjected. "Maybe we'll get a chance to visit with him later."

"I'm sure we will," Adam said, grateful to her for rescuing him. "It's been a pleasure meeting you." They shook hands again.

Both Tara's parents came across as enthusiastic extroverts, Adam reflected as he hurried across the lot to the garage area. Not exactly his type. He had a feeling they could wear him out, but he liked them nevertheless.

ADAM MADE HIS WAY to the garage, again noticing how the condition of the place had deteriorated. From where he was standing, he could see yellow tape blocking off a group of damaged seats in the grandstands. The usable ones around them all looked in dire need of fresh paint.

Only three teams had arrived so far, each using widely scattered bays. They were here only for testing their cars, so the usual rules regarding space limitations didn't apply and they had taken advantage of the vacant stalls beside them to set up spare equipment.

Sanford Racing's No. 483 car gleamed even in the shade, its blue-and-yellow team colors sparkling. Since the hood was up, Adam couldn't see the Greenstone Garden Centers logo emblazoned there, but he could see it on the quarter panel. Trey's crew chief, Ethan Hunt, came over to greet him.

Hunt was a professional in every sense of the word, a man

of integrity who set high standards and accepted nothing less from his crew than complete dedication to the job. Adam appreciated that, but he wasn't blind to the problems it sometimes produced. Ethan Hunt was respected by his team, but he wasn't always liked.

"How's it going?" Adam asked.

"A little slow getting into the rhythm of things," Ethan replied, "but we'll make it. Tire crew's been practicing on the backup car. They're doing better."

The standard for a four-tire change in a pit stop was fourteen seconds. It was demanding work. The slightest deviation from the choreography of a pit stop by a single member, a moment's hesitation or an inadvertent misstep, could cost valuable seconds. Practice was vitally important to get everyone in absolute sync.

"Where's Trey?" Adam asked.

"He thought he was getting a headache, went back to his motor home to take something for it. Offered him some aspirin, but he said he needed something stronger."

Adam didn't like the sound of that, but he would check with his brother later. "I see the Grossos and the Clarks are here."

Andrew Clark founded and owned FastMax Racing, a small team with limited resources. They'd had a few brilliant seasons over the years, made it to the Chase a couple of times, but had never won the NASCAR Sprint Cup Series championship. Late last year Andrew had fired his driver, whose season record was the worst in the series and put his thirty-four-year-old stepson, Garrett Clark, in his place, a move that had been alternately hailed as nepotism, too little too late, a show of desperation and brilliant. The last, decidedly the minority opinion, proved to be the most accurate. Garrett had gone on to win three races and finish in the top five in two more. Too late to make the cut for the Chase for the NASCAR Sprint Cup, but still an incredible achievement. If he maintained that level of skill this year, he would be one of the foremost contenders for the season championship.

"Arrived a few minutes after we did this morning," Hunt replied. "Andrew asked if we wanted to run a couple of trial laps with him tomorrow. I told him I'd check with you."

Andrew Clark was Patsy Grosso's brother. It was well-known that the two didn't get along particularly well, though the specific reason for the friction between them wasn't clear. Sibling rivalry perhaps, but Adam suspected there was more going on. It was none of his business, however. He had a great deal of respect for family privacy.

Adam wondered, though, if Andrew had made the same trial-lap offer to his brother-in-law, Dean.

"Might not be a bad idea," Adam said. "Let's wait and see how we're doing and get Trey's input before we decide."

Ethan nodded his concurrence.

Adam spent the next couple of hours talking to people, observing. As he was walking back to his motor home and thinking about calling Tara, he noticed a tent being erected in a corner of the parking lot beyond the second row of garages and decided to check it out.

The first person he encountered was Juliana Grosso. She was younger than Milo, his second wife of nearly fifty years. In her late seventies, she didn't seem to have slowed down at all since Adam had first met her when he was still a boy trailing after his father. Two other things hadn't changed, either. First, anyone criticizing Milo would have to deal with her, and heaven help the poor son of a gun. Juliana could slice and dice with words sharper than a kitchen knife. Which was the second thing: her cooking. It was legendary.

Her big hair—something else that hadn't changed—a tasteful silver gray, was perfectly in place. She regarded

Adam's approach. The relationship between the two families was something of a conundrum. The accusation that Brent had tried to sabotage Kent was obviously a sore point. That Brent had left NASCAR voluntarily was seen by many as proof of his guilt. At the same time, having to quit NASCAR racing seemed a punishment that more than equaled the crime. So they were at a stalemate. Add to that the fact that Adam had acted reasonably throughout the debacle and Juliana had known him since he was a kid, any hard feelings on a personal level were difficult to maintain.

"What's up?" he asked, scanning the activity around them.

"Only one restaurant left in town." She folded her arms and watched brawny workmen unfolding a heavy canvas. "And it only serves breakfast and lunch now, so I thought I'd fix everybody Italian sausage tomorrow night. Not many people here. Even if a bunch more show up, I'll probably have enough."

"You've never run out of food yet, Juliana. Can't imagine you will this time."

She preened just a little. "Don't want people going hungry."

"Not on your watch. Italian sausage and what?"

"Green peppers and onions on Italian rolls. Macaroni salad on the side. Made tiramisu for dessert, just in case someone wants some."

"Be still, my heart." Adam dramatically clutched his chest. "If you tell people there's tiramisu beforehand, they'll lighten up on eating sausage and peppers so they'll have room for dessert."

"That's the trouble these days," she announced. "Everybody eats so fast, they don't enjoy food the way God intended. If they take their time, there'll be plenty of room for everything."

He chuckled. "I'll keep that in mind."

"A good meal takes hours to eat, not minutes," Juliana insisted, then smiled. "I reckon I'll just wait and surprise them with the tiramisu."

"Good idea." He thought about Tara. "A friend of mine is here—with her parents."

"Bring them along," she said without giving it a second's thought.

"Thanks, Juliana. You're the best."

She sniffed. "You just like my cooking." But there was a twinkle in her eye.

"And I wouldn't know about your cooking, if it weren't for your generosity."

"Sanford. Is that an Irish name? Because you're full of blarney today. No!" she called to a workman who was starting to unload folding chairs from the back of a stake-bed delivery truck. "They go over there." She set off to supervise.

Adam chuckled and continued on his way to his motor home.

He had started across the infield lot when he decided to detour to the flame-red motor home. Tomorrow's dinner was taken care of, but there was still tonight. He mounted the metal steps and knocked on the door.

Shirley opened it within a few seconds. "Oh, Mr. Sanford—"

"Call me Adam, please. Is Tara—"

"Ta-ra!" Shirley bellowed over her shoulder. "Adam's here."

He felt like a high-school kid picking up his date on a Saturday night. His "date" appeared a second later.

"Hi, Adam." She sounded a little sheepish, reinforcing the impression. "Mom, I'll be just outside."

"You take your time, honey. We'll be right here." Guarding. Watching.

Tara stepped onto the tiny metal landing, pulling the door closed behind her.

"I was wondering what your plans were for dinner tonight," Adam said. "There aren't any restaurants open in the evening in Halesboro, but Ashville isn't very far. I thought we might go there."

"Mom was going to fix supper here, but I'm sure she'd much rather eat out and not have to do dishes."

He didn't mean to frown, but he must have.

"Oh." Tara stopped, her keen blue eyes reading his face. "You meant just the two of us."

"They're invited, too, of course," he replied automatically, and wanted to kick himself.

The corners of her mouth turned down, while her eyes twinkled up at him. "I didn't mean to put you on the spot, Adam, honest. Your invitation is very nice. Thank you, but—"

"You haven't. I need to shower and change clothes. Tell your folks I'll pick y'all up in an hour."

Tara laughed, a bubbly little sound that made him want to pick her up in his arms and twirl her around. "We'll be ready." She placed her hands on his biceps, rose on tiptoe and kissed him sweetly on the lips. Instinct had him reaching for her, but she pulled away before he could complete the action. "Thanks, Adam, for being such a good sport. We'll be ready." She bounded up the metal stairs and was inside before he could utter another word.

He licked his lips on his way to his motor home. *Maybe,* he consoled himself along the way, *we can share dessert afterward...privately, at my place.*

TARA WAS WORRIED about how the evening would go. Her parents could be overwhelming at times. More than one boyfriend had practically fled screaming after spending a few hours with them. Tara had to admit none of them was probably a great loss, but unfortunately Spenser had made it through the gauntlet.

"I can't believe I'll be going to dinner with the owner of Sanford Racing!" Shirley exclaimed for the umpteenth time as she sat at her vanity, applying a fresh layer of makeup. She was adding the finishing touches to her mascara when Adam knocked on the door.

They went in his SUV. Tara sat in front beside him, her parents holding hands in the backseat. Tara kept glancing at the man behind the wheel to get his reaction to them. She hadn't missed the occasional twitch at the corner of his mouth when he suppressed a grin.

"I ran into Garrett Clark today," Shirley announced, "and talked to him for a few minutes. Can you imagine? I had a conversation with Garrett Clark, like he was an ordinary person."

Tara sighed internally and decided to play the straight man. "What did you talk about, Mom?" She wondered if Adam was buying the fan rave.

"He's worried about the weather," her mother said. "It's warm for January. He hopes it stays that way, because a cold snap would change the way his car performs, so the testing they're doing wouldn't be valid. I already knew that, of course, but…"

Adam was headed for a steakhouse when Shirley pointed to a vegetarian restaurant on the other side of the road. He immediately did a U-turn and pulled into the parking lot.

An hour and half later, after Adam had insisted on picking up the tab, he and Tara were walking behind her parents to his vehicle. She leaned into him and whispered, "Was dinner so bad?"

"Actually, it was very good." He raised his voice enough for the couple ahead of them to hear. "Too bad your folks are vegetarians, though."

Buddy stopped and turned around. "Why do you say that?"

"It's just that I had a dinner invitation for you and your

wife for tomorrow night, but I wouldn't want to embarrass you or cause the hosts discomfort."

"What kind of an invitation?" Shirley asked, all interest.

"Well," Adam said with some reluctance, "I ran into Juliana Grosso this afternoon, and she invited all of us to her cook-out tomorrow evening. She's fixing Italian sausage for anyone who's still here. Sausage with green peppers and onions on her homemade Italian rolls."

"Sausage and peppers. Yeoowie," Buddy let rip.

"With the Grossos?" Shirley asked, awestruck.

"And the Clarks and us Sanfords, of course. I know Tara eats meat, so I assumed you folks did, too. I should have checked with you first. Sorry. I'll let Juliana know you can't make it."

"We eat meat," Shirley blurted. "I just wasn't in the mood for it tonight. Turn down Juliana Grosso's cooking? Why, I wouldn't think of it. Of course, we accept her kind invitation."

"I LIKE HIM," Shirley told Tara a little while later.

Tara snickered. "He called your bluff."

"Well—"

"He did," Buddy agreed. "He beared with us this evening, so he's all right."

"Run along, dear," Shirley said, "and don't worry about disturbing us when you come in. We'll be sound asleep."

Tara shook her head and left for Adam's motor home. She mounted the broad metal steps with a pretty good idea of what to expect inside, but when he let her in, she was nevertheless stunned by what she found. This was nothing like her parents' motor home. The plush interior had undoubtedly been professionally custom-designed to reflect Adam's taste—traditional furniture, yet bold in color and texture. Discreet, indirect lighting. A wide-screen plasma television dominating one wall. A malachite marble-top bar separating the living area from the fully equipped kitchen.

"How did you know they weren't vegetarians?" she asked after accepting the glass of wine he offered.

He grinned and wrapped his arms around her hips. "Your father didn't know how to pronounce ratatouille."

She turned into his embrace and murmured, "Thank you for putting up with them."

"Speaking of putting up—" he tightened the body contact between them "—I've been wanting to kiss you all evening."

"The evening isn't over," she reminded him.

He took the glass he'd just given her, placed it on the counter behind her, folded her again into his arms and placed his lips on hers. The kiss that followed was intense and thorough. When at last he broke off, they were both breathless. He gazed into her eyes, and she felt as if she were being drawn into the emerald-green depths of his. "Will you spend the night with me, Tara?"

Her pulse raced. She recalled his earlier words: *Think very carefully about your answer.* She was about to cross a line, one she couldn't cross back. If this were just a matter of physical attraction, the answer would be easy…easier. But it was more than physical attraction, as strong as that was. If she spent the night with Adam, tomorrow would be different. All her tomorrows would be different. She would be different.

She smiled into his eyes. "Yes."

CHAPTER TWELVE

TREY SANFORD, Kent Grosso and Garrett Clark had been test-driving all morning, working with their teams to adjust engine settings, experiment with front and rear suspension systems, determine optimum tire pressures. Each driver generally ignored the other cars on the track, giving one another a wide berth.

After lunch, however, the atmosphere changed. Competitive instincts took hold and the three drivers demonstrated awareness of each other.

"Do you think they're going to race?" Shirley asked Tara. They were sitting in the stands across from the garage-area entrance onto pit road.

"I don't know," Tara admitted. Usually at test tracks there were more cars competing for space, so impromptu races were not possible. "With just the three of them here..."

Kent Grosso zoomed by at cruise speed on the outside, his cousin, Garrett Clark, on his tail. Trey Sanford flew up behind him, then quickly slid to the right and passed him.

Instantly Garrett was on his bumper, giving him a draft, and the two went gliding past Kent, who was still on the outside lane.

Suddenly the three were playing a sort of leapfrog, the trailing two passing the lead, the former lead then giving the second car a draft and passing the new leader. They repeated this pattern for several laps.

It was fun to watch, and it seemed clear the participants were enjoying themselves, until Garrett, in the middle position, got tapped by Kent from behind and began to rotate toward the outside wall between turns Three and Four. The steepness of the banking saved him from slamming into the wall.

Garrett recovered, but barely, his right rear quarter panel brushing the barrier.

"Uh-oh," Buddy muttered. "I don't think that was in the game plan. Body-repair time."

Tara shifted her attention to the pit area, where owners and teams were watching. She saw Andrew Clark say something to Dean Grosso. From the expressions on their faces it wasn't friendly. Things seemed to be getting acrimonious when Adam wedged himself between them.

More words were traded between the two brothers-in-law, then Adam said something and the altercation stopped. The two team owners turned independently back to the track and the three cars streamed by in spaced-out single file. Clark shook his head. Dean put his hand on his shoulder, said something in his ear, smiled and walked away.

"I wonder what Adam told them," Shirley said.

"We'll probably never know," Tara said, "and it's none of our business." Though she had every intention of asking as soon as she got a chance.

Her mother glanced at her for a moment, then redirected her attention to the track.

The cars took turns coming in to pit road to their designated spots, where they gassed up and changed tires, while the crew chief stood by with stopwatch in hand, timing them. They continued to race for another hour and a half before finally calling it quits.

Tara and her parents were allowed in the garage area afterward but were careful to stay out of the way. Adam joined them.

"What did you say to Clark and Grosso that calmed them down?" she asked him.

Adam raised an eyebrow at the question. "I explained that you were here, watching, and that you were writing a book."

Her jaw dropped. Did he really say that? More importantly, did he still see her as the enemy? Even after last night?

He chuckled. "Actually, I told them Juliana would probably send them both to bed without dinner tonight if they weren't good little boys."

Tara couldn't help but laugh. She also wondered if either statement was true. Okay, he'd made his point. As she'd told her parents earlier, it was none of her business. Why would he even joke about her being the equivalent of a spy if the thought wasn't on his mind?

Knock off the paranoia, she told herself. *Stop checking for a cloud in the silver lining.*

TARA'S FOLKS decided they needed to rest up before their exciting evening hobnobbing with the NASCAR elite, so they returned to their motor home for a nap. That left Tara free to wander around and talk to people, pick up information and impressions she could use in her book. This might also be a good time to try for an interview with Trey.

She spied him entering the hauler after No. 483 and its backup had been loaded in the overhead compartment. Track protocol kept haulers off-limits to the media, but as she tried to impress upon Adam, she wasn't part of the media. Besides, she'd been personally invited to attend this testing session by the team owner himself. Still, given Adam's preoccupation with privacy, this invasion held an element of danger.

Taking a fortifying breath, she strolled up the long narrow aisle between the rows of tool-storage bins to the lounge, expecting to find Trey alone. She was about to call out, to announce her presence, when she heard voices. Trey's and Adam's. She stopped short.

"I'm flying out from Dallas tomorrow night," Trey stated forcefully.

"This is a bad time," Adam warned. "Can't you put it off? A couple of blogs have been talking about your dead-of-night trips. Apparently someone saw you at the airstrip. Speculation is rife, and you know what damage that can do. Tara has figured out you go to Mexico. She even asked if you're running drugs."

Tara heard the *pfft* sound of a cap being twisted off a soft-drink bottle. "What did you tell her?" Trey sounded more amused than shocked.

"What do you think I told her?" Adam responded sarcastically. "Look, wait a little while longer, until the curiosity wanes?"

"I have to go now," Trey insisted. "I have no choice. Supplies are running low, and I don't want to take a chance on a local purchase. Talk about speculation. If word of that ever got out…"

"Just be careful," Adam warned. "If anyone discovers…"

Tara backed away and all but tiptoed down the aisle, continually glancing back over her shoulder, her heart pounding. At the trailer's opening she looked around, feeling like a sneak. No one in view. She was shaking so badly she almost tripped as she stepped down onto the stained concrete pad.

What had she just overheard? What did it mean? And what would happen when she asked Adam about it?

Willing the tension to subside, Tara wandered over to the tent that had been erected. Its sides were still rolled up from when long tables and folding chairs had been brought in. The air was perfectly still, pleasantly warmed by the afternoon sun. In another hour, as darkness gathered, winter's chill would set in, the flaps would have to come down and the space heaters, already positioned in the four corners, lighted. Beyond the perimeter of the tent stood a couple of drum barbecue pits, hickory kindling peeking over the edges, waiting for a match. Nearby was a stack of larger pieces of firewood.

Tara had hoped she would find Juliana Grosso there and the two of them could talk. She imagined the older woman had plenty of tales to tell. Probably taking a nap, too. Tara decided she ought to, as well.

She was passing Adam's motor home when she heard him call her name. She spun around, unsure what to expect. Had he seen her at the hauler? Had he been waiting for her to pass by so he could lecture her in private?

"I was hoping I'd find you." He had a smile on his face. "How about an aperitif?"

She told herself to relax. He hadn't seen her. She forced herself to smile. "What kind of aperitif?"

He laughed. "Premium beer and eight-year-old bourbon whiskey. I also have white and red wine. How about it?"

"The sun is over the yardarm," she said, "and below the mountain top."

She accepted a glass of chilled white wine and sat on the hunter-green leather couch. He sat beside her and encircled her with his arm, then pulled her snugly against his chest. She didn't resist. In fact, she cuddled against his solid body, remembering all too well the sight, scent and texture of his skin against hers the night before. She could hear his heartbeat, slow, strong and steady.

"Your folks doing okay?" he asked.

She let out a breath. "They're ecstatic, Adam. Thank you for being so kind to them."

"They're fun people. I like them."

She chuckled. "Fun can be exhausting. They can be exhausting."

He kissed her temple. "They're good people. That's what's important."

He was a good person, too, who deserved honesty. She extracted herself from his grasp and rose to her feet. He looked up and questioned her with his eyes.

"A little while ago—" she paced in front of him "—I followed Trey into the hauler. I was hoping I could talk him into an interview. He didn't know I was behind him. I overheard the two of you talking. Only for a minute," she clarified, "but it was enough for me to realize he's flying to Mexico tomorrow night and you don't want him to." She stared down at him. "Why, Adam? If he only visits friends and goes fishing there, why did you say it was dangerous?"

"Did I?" He tilted his head back and drew his brows together, gazing up at the ceiling, not at her. His chest rose and fell. "I don't remember saying that," he murmured, finally making eye contact, challenging her.

"Perhaps not those exact words," she admitted, trying hard not to feel intimidated, "but you weren't pleased that he's flying there, because people might be watching. You wanted him to postpone the trip if he could. What is it he doesn't want to buy locally, Adam?"

His complexion darkened. She waited for him to jump angrily to his feet, maybe order her to leave, but he stayed where he was, even extended his arm, as if casually, across the back of the couch.

"Sounds like you heard more than a moment's worth." His tone was level, but it didn't quite mask his pique. "And you seem to have inferred a lot from what little you did overhear."

She studied him, his firm jaw, the sadness—or was it disappointment?—in his eyes.

"I wasn't intentionally spying on you or your brother," she protested. "I want you to know that, but you're not answering my question."

A long moment passed in silence. "Do you remember our first conversation?" He peered up at her. "You said you were interested in the human-interest angle, and I said, with all respect, that what you might consider human interest, I might consider none of your business."

She pursed her lips in frustration. "I remember."

"So I'll ask you again, Tara. Do you think Trey is smuggling drugs?" She could see the pulse in his neck throbbing, the only indication that he wasn't as calm as his tone suggested. "Do you think I am involved with him in the illegal narcotics trade?"

"No, of course not."

Now he did rise, but he maintained his distance from her. "There's no *of course* about it, Tara," he declared very seriously. "You've considered the possibility that I am trafficking in illegal substances. You've told me so." He stared into her eyes with such fierceness, he almost scared her. "So I have to ask you again, Tara, and I need an absolutely honest answer, one you can live with without reservation. Do you believe that Trey or I are involved in any way with narcotics?"

Her head told her that all the facts weren't in, that what information she had was ambiguous, that there was no evidence to contradict the allegations. But her heart told her something else. Adam could be domineering, unreasonably demanding, temperamental, but he wasn't dishonest. Yes, he almost scared her, but the operative word was *almost*.

She shook her head. "No, I don't."

"You're absolutely sure?"

"I'm absolutely sure," she repeated, not flinching from his intense scrutiny.

"Good." He visibly relaxed, closed the gap between them and drew her into his arms. He held her for a time before she finally leaned back, looked up at him and asked, "If I had been less certain, Adam, less than absolute in my answer, what would have happened?"

"We still would have drunk our wine and I would have taken you and your folks to enjoy Juliana's Italian-sausage supper," he said mischievously. When he saw she wasn't smiling, he added, "Then I would have ended our relationship."

"You wouldn't have tried to convince me otherwise?"

He rubbed her back soothingly with his hands, large, capable, sure hands. "It would have been pointless, Tara. It's sort of like Brent's dilemma. The more he tried to defend himself against the sabotage charges, the guiltier he looked. No one can prove a negative. I'd do the same thing he did, even though I didn't agree with what he did at the time. I'd walk away."

He was telling the truth. It filled her with dread to know that, despite what they'd shared the night before, he had the willpower, the self-discipline to act on what he said.

"You're not going to tell me why Trey flies to Mexico, are you?"

"I've already told you. To visit friends and go fishing." He looked directly into her eyes. "Don't you believe me?"

She studied his features, so strong and handsome. "No."

He laughed. "Let Trey be Trey, and you and I be us." He kissed her gently. "I like *us.*"

They settled onto the couch again and snuggled in silence. Encircled in his embrace, she was content to listen to the relentless rhythm of his heart. It wasn't until he shifted that she roused. She'd fallen asleep! In his arms. He was withholding a secret from her, being less than completely honest, yet she was strangely at peace with him. For now, at least.

It wouldn't do as a definition of love, but there was something about the feelings he stirred in her that came close.

TARA USED Adam's bathroom to freshen up, then they went together to her parents' motor home. Shirley looked dazed when she answered the door, and Tara realized they'd awakened her. Buddy was still snoring on the couch. A swipe of his wife's hand on his foot roused him. He blinked and smiled.

"I guess I was more tired than I thought." He rubbed his eyes.

"Give me ten minutes to put on my face," Shirley said, "and we'll be right with you."

On his feet now, Buddy remarked behind his hand, "That would be a world record. It took her twenty minutes forty years ago, and we've both slowed down since then. Not stopped, mind you—" he winked at Adam "—just slowed the pace."

"We have more time now," Shirley agreed, apparently not in the least offended by his remark. She slipped into the small bathroom. "There's a lot to be said for slowing down, isn't there, Buddy?"

"Amen."

Shirley laughed at the expression on her daughter's face and shut the door.

Twenty-five minutes later the four of them stepped outside into the cool, damp night air and started toward the floodlit tent. The aroma of hickory smoke and Italian spices filled the air.

The crowded tent was warm and noisy. Most of those in attendance were men. Adam assumed the role of host and took his guests around to introduce them. First he sought out Juliana and Milo.

The older woman had a white bib apron wrapped around her trim figure.

"Thank you so much for inviting us," Shirley said. "Your cooking is famous."

"We're privileged to get to taste it," Buddy added. He turned to Milo, who was several inches shorter and a great deal lighter in build. "Mr. Grosso, it is truly an honor to meet you. My father was at Daytona for your first NASCAR race, and I was with him fifteen years later when you won your last race there, just before you retired. I'll never forget the way you edged out Kiefer Reynolds coming out of Turn Four."

"A lot of people didn't think I could do it, but I did," the old-timer crowed.

"You've gotten him started." Juliana smiled indulgently. "Now you're in for it."

"Milo," Adam interrupted, "let me take them around to meet the others, then I'll bring them back. I promise."

The living legend snorted. "Nobody wants to hear about the old days anymore."

"I do," Buddy told him. "You talk and I'll listen."

Adam introduced them to Dean and Patsy Grosso. Again, Tara watched Adam. He seemed genuinely amused by her parents' chameleonlike abilities. Last night they had been loud and boisterous. This evening they were reserved and dignified. Adam winked conspiratorially at Tara.

The introductions went easily since the Daltons recognized nearly everyone and made appropriate comments that immediately won them over.

Tapping on a pot with a wooden spoon, loud enough to be heard over the din of conversation and laughter, Juliana got everyone's attention and announced it was time to eat.

Tara managed to position herself immediately behind Trey on the buffet line.

"How's the fishing?" she asked.

He spun around, a ready smile on his face. If she thought she was going to catch him off guard, she was underestimating him, she realized. Adam had probably warned him she was on his case.

"Ever been to San Meloso? It's an angler's paradise."

Juliana cackled from the other side of the long serving table. "Girl, if you think he flies south of the border to go fishing, you're out of your mind. I bet it's a woman."

Trey looked at Tara with a sly grin and winked.

Tara chuckled to herself. Her first instinct had been right. Look for the woman.

"Or it's to try to convince Roberto Castillo to race in NASCAR," Dean observed from in front of Trey. "Any luck in that department?"

Trey smiled and put a third sausage link on his plate beside the huge mound of macaroni salad he'd already helped himself to. Tara noted that he didn't answer Dean, and Dean didn't press him.

The assembly quieted down as people began to eat. Tara had hoped to sit with Dean and Patsy Grosso, but by the time she'd filled her plate, the couple was surrounded by team members. Adam made room for her at his table. An hour later, after everyone had had at least a sample of Juliana's tiramisu, people were gathered around Milo while Buddy prompted him to talk about races many of them had never even heard of. The old man was in his glory, and Buddy was smiling like a proud papa.

"Your folks are something else," Adam commented later, after he and Tara had seen them to their motor home. Shirley had been a bit mellow after two glasses of red wine. Buddy was still sober as a judge after three. "Your dad certainly made a hit with Milo."

"Believe me, the adulation was sincere," Tara said. "They've always been Grosso fans, no offense intended," she added.

Adam snorted. "None taken. If I weren't a Sanford, I might be a Grosso fan, too."

It was an interesting admission. They strolled on, hand in hand, toward his motor home. When they arrived, he said nonchalantly, "Oh, I almost forgot. I have some news for you."

She gawked over at him, suddenly nervous. "What?"

"I talked with Dean and Patsy this evening. They've agreed to let you interview them."

Her mouth fell open.

He laughed. "They said if you come to their farm in Mooresville—I can give you the directions, if you don't know where it is—they'll give you an hour or so."

"Adam, that's wonderful, fantastic. Thank you. How can I ever make it up to you?"

He grinned. "Oh, I'll think of something."

CHAPTER THIRTEEN

THE GROSSO FARMHOUSE, nicknamed Villa Grosso, was not visible from the road. Tara was expected, so there was no delay when she pressed the call button on the control panel set into the left stone pillar of the formal entrance. The large, wrought-iron gates swung open, and she proceeded up a wide blacktop through a wooded area. At the end of a gentle curve the house came into view, a sprawling, Southern-style plantation house. She pulled up the circular driveway in front of the broad open porch.

A middle-aged woman with perfectly groomed russet-colored hair, wearing a black-and-white uniform, answered the ring of the bell.

"Good morning. I'm Tara Dalton—" Tara started.

"Thank you, Clarice." Milo Grosso walked up behind her. "I'll take care of Miss Dalton."

"Yes, sir."

"Come in, come in," Milo invited Tara with a warm smile. As the older woman disappeared into a room on the left, he remarked, "Hired her when my wife went into the hospital for her gallbladder surgery and decided to keep her on. She does the housework and Juliana does the cooking. How's your dad?"

He led her down the central "breezeway" to the kitchen, where Juliana was busy snapping green beans.

"He's fine," Tara answered. "They're up in Virginia now, checking out a couple of practice tracks there."

"Nice folks. Give them our best." He climbed cautiously onto a stool at the massive black-granite counter opposite his wife and grabbed a freshly rinsed bean from the colander.

"I will," Tara said. "They were really thrilled to meet you both."

"Dean and Patsy will be with you in just a couple of minutes," Juliana informed her. "Patsy's in the greenhouse, and Dean's out in the garage. You want some coffee? I made a fresh pot."

"Thank you, but I've had my quota for today."

"I hope you like lentils, because we're having hot lentil salad for lunch. You'll stay, I hope."

"Thank you. As long as I'm not imposing." Tara took a stool next to Milo and reached for a string bean to contribute to the effort.

"Since we have a couple of minutes alone," she said, "maybe you can help me with something. I'd like to ask your grandson and his wife about Gina, and I'm hoping you might give me some advice on how to approach the subject."

Milo stopped what he was doing and eyed his wife.

"How do you know about Gina?" Juliana asked guardedly.

"Her name was mentioned on a Web site for missing and exploited children," Tara explained.

Juliana projected her jaw and shook her head, whether it was in disapproval of the Internet or Tara's interest, Tara wasn't clear. "Whyever would you want to even bring up such a painful subject?"

Tara realized she'd stepped out on a tightrope. "I know it's difficult to talk about," she acknowledged. "That's why I'm hoping you can help me. The book I'm writing is about overcoming problems, moving on. Dean and Patsy—and you all—have obviously done that. It couldn't have been easy. That you've been able to keep going, stay positive and be successful is inspiring. I want to tell readers—"

"It's none of their damn business," Milo snarled heatedly.

"Calm down, honey," Juliana cautioned him. Her hands continued to work as if of their own accord, but her lips tightened, bringing out age lines she didn't normally display. Her displeasure was palpable. "Gina is not missing, Tara," she insisted. "She's dead."

The statement was like a shotgun blast.

They continued snapping beans in silence for another minute. Tara decided she'd gone this far; it was too late to retreat.

"I know that's what everyone believes," she said sympathetically, "and that it's probably true, but according to a blog I've read, Gina's not only still alive, she's connected to NASCAR."

Juliana stopped what she was doing this time and visibly seethed. "That's ridiculous. How dare you go spreading rumors like that."

"I'm not spreading them," Tara said in an attempt to defend herself. "I'm trying to find out if they're true."

Juliana didn't seem to have heard her. "Do you have any idea what you're doing, dredging this up?" she erupted anew. "How dare you come into this house and stir up such unbearable pain. Leave it alone, young lady. I'm warning you. Don't you dare mention that poor, sweet child's name again, not here, not now, not ever. Do you hear me? Never!"

"I'm sorry." Tara was shaken by the elderly woman's vehemence. "I didn't mean—"

"Never," Juliana repeated, her rage undiminished by her guest's apology.

"I won't," Tara said. If the child's great-grandmother felt this strongly about the subject, how much more painful must it be for the parents? "I'm sorry," she repeated. "I didn't mean to upset you. I promise not to mention her."

Juliana glared at her and only gradually calmed down. Tara realized she'd probably lost a potential friend, and that saddened her. She'd known the subject would be difficult, but she hadn't anticipated so violent a reaction.

Patsy was the first to appear in the big country kitchen about five minutes later, coming in from an outside door.

"Hi, Tara." She stripped off her work gloves and rinsed her hands at the sink. "Glad you could make it." She seemed blessedly unaware of the tension in the room.

Tara strained to act naturally, at ease. "Thank you so much for agreeing to see me."

Patsy poured herself a cup of coffee. "Let's go into the den. Dean should be here in a minute, and we can get started."

Tara knew enough about gardening to inquire about the varieties of plants and flowers Patsy was nurturing—small talk, intended to relax them before they got started on the interview.

The den was a large room with a pool table at one end, an old upright piano in a corner, a dartboard and card table, in addition to a large-screen TV and professional sound system. Patsy waved Tara to the couch in front of the blank screen and took a nearby armchair for herself. They were just getting settled when Dean joined them. He was wearing jeans and a dark green polo shirt.

Tara dove right in. They talked about Kent's performance last season with Maximus Motorsports and expectations for his coming season with Cargill-Grosso Racing, as well as the considerations that went into his transfer of teams. They compared his driving record with his father's at the same point in Dean's career and discussed Dean's new role as an owner.

"You're a partner in this enterprise," Tara said to Patsy. "Do you intend to take an active role in managing the business?"

"I'll let Dean handle most of the PR—unless he makes a mistake and I have to correct him, of course." She slanted her husband a wry grin. "He's had more experience in front of a camera than I have, and he's more comfortable there."

"Boy, have I fooled you," he rejoined lightly and addressed Tara. "We'll make decisions together. We always have, anyway, so this will be nothing new."

"I understand you're keeping the Cargill name," Tara said.

"We'll be Cargill-Grosso Racing from now on," Patsy replied. "We've also asked Alan's son, Nathan, to stay on as general manager during the transition."

"And we're very happy he's agreed," Dean added.

"Do the police have any idea yet who killed Alan or why?" Tara asked.

Dean shook his head. "Robbery, probably. As for who…" He shrugged. "If the police have any suspects, they haven't said anything to us."

"We're hoping they'll make an arrest soon. It'll be hard to bring closure until they do."

It was the perfect opening to mention Gina. How had they reached closure after their baby was taken? How long did it take them? But Tara had made a promise to Juliana.

"Alan Cargill told Adam Sanford after the banquet that he had new information that cast doubt on Brent's involvement in the sabotage four years ago. What was he referring to?"

Dean didn't know. "He never said anything about it to me."

"Any idea why he didn't?"

"We hadn't seen each other in several days," Dean responded. "He wasn't one for long telephone conversations, discussing business or personal matters on the phone. I imagine he was just waiting until we had a chance to meet face-to-face."

"Or," Patsy suggested, "he'd received the information so recently that he hadn't had time to talk to us about it yet."

"That may be why he didn't want to go into detail with Adam that night," Dean said. "Because he hadn't had a chance to talk to us about it yet."

"I wish he had," Patsy murmured.

Tara had wondered if there was any significance to the fact

that Alan had mentioned having new information to Adam Sanford at the banquet but not to his team's new owners, who were also his close friends. Maybe it was just a matter of opportunity. He probably planned to talk to the Grossos about it later at the party. He wasn't likely to run into Adam again that evening and so he wanted to let him know Brent might be off the hook.

None of this, of course, answered the central questions: what had he known at the banquet that he hadn't known before? And did it have anything to do with his being killed?

At the end of an hour and a half, her hosts had been so forthcoming and at ease with her that Tara wondered if she might still be able to bring up the subject of Gina. Again, she told herself no. Breaking her word to Juliana was wrong. Besides, there would probably be other opportunities.

She'd already stayed well into a second hour when Dean's stomach growled.

"Thank you so much for your time—" Tara stood up "—and for your candid answers to my questions."

"Can you stay for lunch?" Patsy asked as she and her husband got up.

She hesitated. Tara wasn't sure she'd still be welcome, and she certainly didn't want to upset the matriarch of the family any more than she already had.

"That's very kind of you," she said. "Juliana invited me, too, and I thought I could stay, but I've already taken up too much of your time, and I'm running late for another appointment." Which was technically true, but she could have changed it with a phone call. They headed toward the front door. "Please thank Juliana and say goodbye to her and Milo for me."

"Good luck with the book," Dean said.

"THAT WENT WELL enough," Patsy said as she and her husband entered the kitchen.

"Lunch in a few minutes," Juliana announced. "Wash up."

Dean suppressed a snicker. His grandmother's mothering hadn't let up, even though he and Patsy had been married more than thirty years. She acted sometimes like they were still teenagers. Maybe that was a compliment, he thought with a grin.

"Where's Tara?" Juliana turned off the gas under a pot. "I set a place for her, too." Steam rose as she removed the lid.

"We talked much longer than either of us expected. She said to thank you, but she was running behind schedule."

"She didn't mention Gina, did she?" Milo asked.

Juliana dropped the serving spoon she was using to dish up the hot lentil salad. "Milo," she muttered anxiously.

He closed his eyes and sucked air between his teeth.

"What did you say?" Patsy asked, suddenly on high alert.

"Damn that girl," Juliana groaned as she bent down and retrieved the fallen implement.

"Milo?" Dean questioned when his grandfather didn't reply.

"What's going on?" Patsy demanded.

Juliana removed a clean serving spoon from a drawer. "Sit down and eat your lunch," she ordered.

"The hell with lunch, Nana," Patsy snapped, clearly upset. "Answer me. What did Tara say about Gina?"

"Honey—" Dean tried to put an arm around her "—calm down."

Patsy shook him off. "Tell me, dammit," Patsy ordered Juliana.

"Don't you dare speak to my wife that way," Milo exploded, his face red, his arthritic fists shaking.

Patsy turned to him and was about to lash out at him, too, until she saw how agitated he was. Dean watched her rein in her emotions. "I'm sorry," she murmured more calmly. "Just tell me what's going on. What did Tara say?" When neither of her in-laws spoke up, she persisted, "I'm waiting."

"She was going to ask you about Gina," Juliana blurted.

"What? Why?"

The elderly woman put down the spoon she'd been wielding, splayed her hands across the countertop and hung her head for a moment. "She said Gina's name came up on some Internet Web site or blog or whatever they call it about missing children. Somebody said she's alive and works for NASCAR. I told her Gina wasn't missing. She's—"

"Juliana, shut up," Milo said, then went around the counter and rubbed her back. "Honey—"

"I wish you had," his wife replied without recrimination, her eyes moist with tears.

"She's alive?" Patsy mumbled, then nearly whimpered. "If somebody knows something about her… If…"

Dean moved to her side. This time she let him enfold her in his arms. "Let it go, sweetheart. Let it go."

"But if—"

"Patsy, we went through all this years ago. Please don't make us go through it again. We know what happened. It's done, finished. Over. Let it go."

She pulled away, her eyes already red, tears drenching her face. "I can't, Dean!" she cried. "I know you think Gina is dead, but I've never believed it. She was my baby. If someone knows something…"

"After all these years?" he asked incredulously, trying to disguise his anger. "If she had survived… This is just someone trying to stir up trouble. For all we know, Tara made it up, just to get a rise out of us."

"Well, she certainly succeeded," Juliana grumbled.

"To stir things up for her book," Dean continued. "She wouldn't be the first writer to invent stories."

"She wouldn't do that. She could have asked us," Patsy said.

"I forbade her to say anything," Juliana stated.

Patsy countered, "Nana, if she was such a terrible person, she wouldn't have obeyed you." She wrung her hands. "I can't just let it go, Dean." It was as much a plea as a statement. "Please don't ask me to. She was my baby."

"She was my baby, too, dammit." He thrust out his jaw. "Do you think I didn't feel anything when she was taken? That I…"

This time Patsy came to him. She rested her hand on his taut arm. "I know you do," she murmured. "That's why we have to make sure. If someone is saying she's still alive, we have to know why. We have to check it out."

He turned his head away. Even after three decades the thought of his baby being taken ached so hard his stomach hurt.

Patsy was right. They had to know for sure. His first impulse was to find Tara and confront her, but he didn't trust himself to be rational if he did. If NASCAR racing had taught him anything over the years, it was not to act emotionally. There was no surer way to lose a race than stomping on the gas pedal in a fit of temper. If, by a remote chance—he was afraid to contemplate the possibility—Tara had been telling the truth, that Gina was still alive, he didn't want to jeopardize the prospect of finding her by alienating someone who could help them. If, on the other hand, Tara was fabricating the whole thing, there would be time enough to settle his score with her.

"Okay," he finally relented. "I'll call Jake and ask him to look into it."

ADAM PUT DOWN the phone. Tara had shown up at the Villa Grosso as scheduled for her interview and had asked about Gina, Kent's twin sister. Adam hadn't even known Kent *had* a twin sister. According to Dean, the baby girl had been kidnapped shortly after she was born in a hospital in Nashville and, according to the police, had subsequently died or was killed in Mexico—a tragedy that had nearly destroyed Patsy, and from what Adam could glean from the sound of Dean's voice on the phone, nearly destroyed him, as well.

To make matters worse, Tara told them there was a rumor going around the Internet that Gina hadn't really died, that she was alive and somehow connected to NASCAR. None of it made a great deal of sense, but Adam had been reluctant to ask a lot of questions for clarification.

The underlying problem was clear enough. Tara had used her welcome to reopen a painful wound in the Grosso family. Dean hadn't said it in so many words, but it was patently obvious: he thought Adam had set them up with this interview, payback for Brent.

Adam almost laughed at the ridiculousness of the idea, then felt outrage that Dean would even imply that he would stoop so low as to use a dead child to undermine his opponent's confidence. Fortunately, before he flew into a rage at him, Adam realized how devastating the issue had to be for the man to make such an over-the-top accusation.

Adam had made a mistake when he'd agreed to give Belinda Goddard an interview. He'd thought at the time it was an innocent opportunity for positive PR. He'd had doubts about Tara from the beginning. Had he let physical attraction and sweet words lull him into a false sense of trust? Had he once again been betrayed?

CHAPTER FOURTEEN

PATSY AND DEAN went to the Cotton Gin, a quiet, upscale restaurant near Concord. As the name implied, the unimpressive tin building had once housed a cotton gin, but it had been gutted of the huge, deafening machinery used in extracting seed from fiber decades earlier, when cotton had ceased to be king in the Old South. The central area was now a spacious dining room, the walkways and ancillary chambers converted to private dining areas. It was in one of these upper alcoves that they met Jake McMasters.

A former Special Forces operative, Patsy's cousin was a year or two younger than Dean, with sandy-brown hair and light blue eyes. He'd stood six-one in his physical heyday, but the injury that had mandated his retirement obliged him to use a cane. Leaning on it robbed him of the impression of height. It also made him appear harmless, the type of guy you passed on the street without really noticing. Since he now ran his own private investigative service, that unthreatening anonymity had become one of his greatest assets. People felt safe telling him things they normally wouldn't confide to a stranger. And he never gave up on an assignment.

"Thanks for joining us." Dean extended his hand.

Jake took it, reciprocated the manly grip, then turned to Patsy. She gave him a peck on the cheek.

"And on such short notice," she reminded him. Dean had spoken to him on the phone only that afternoon.

"Congratulations on becoming the new owners of a NASCAR Sprint Cup Series team," Jake said. "Milo must be ecstatic. I was sorry to hear about your friend Alan Cargill, though."

Dean ordered a martini from the waitress. Patsy requested a frozen daiquiri. Jake was content with the beer he already had.

"Is Cargill's death what you wanted to see me about?" Jake asked after the waitress had left.

Dean shook his head. "Actually, no."

"It's about Gina," Patsy blurted impatiently.

Jake didn't startle easily, but it was clear she'd caught him by surprise. "Kent's twin?"

No one had talked about Gina in years. Yet the baby girl Patsy had gotten to hold only a few minutes was never too far below the surface of her thoughts, her emotions. Hot embers buried below years of ash, waiting to be stirred to life, and Tara had done just that.

"There's a rumor on the Internet," Dean told him, "that she's alive and that she's nearby. She's even supposed to be involved with NASCAR in some way."

Their drinks arrived. They ordered from the food menu. Again Jake waited until they were alone before continuing.

"There's a lot of crap on the Internet," he observed. "How can you be sure someone isn't just trying to make mischief? Cruel mischief, but—"

"That's the point," Patsy said. "We don't. We need you to find out what's going on."

Jake picked up his glass of beer and took a thoughtful sip.

"I'd just graduated high school when all this happened," he reminded them. "Mom told me about the kidnapping, but I was preoccupied with trying to get into West Point at the time. Please review the case for me?"

Patsy took a deep breath. "We were just kids, too. Dean

was eighteen and driving in the NASCAR's weekly series at the time. I was seventeen and eight and a half months pregnant."

"We'd gotten married sooner than we'd planned," Dean admitted, "because of the baby, and even with help from our families we were struggling to makes ends meet."

"But it was an exciting time. We were crazy in love with each other." Patsy reached for his hand.

"I'd been having a good season." Dean gently squeezed her fingers. "My best performance till then. Finished in the top five for the last six races. I'd taken the checkered flag twice."

Patsy took over. "We were in Nashville. Dean had run his second best-ever lap in a practice heat when I went into labor. He rushed me to the local hospital. We were excited, scared." She looked over at her husband. "When we got there, he didn't want to leave my side. Kept holding my hand—" like he was doing now "—assuring me everything was going to be all right."

"Men weren't allowed in the delivery room in those days," Dean said, "so I was banished to the waiting room. Two hours of torture later, she gave birth to a little boy. We named him Kent after her dad. Then, wonder of wonders, a surprise beyond our imaginings—"

"I gave birth to a little girl ten minutes later. We named her Gina after Dean's late mother. Two perfect little lives."

"We'd gone from just the two of us," Dean said with what was almost a smile, "to a family of four in a matter of minutes."

"And we couldn't have been happier," Patsy emphasized.

"The twins were born late Wednesday afternoon," Dean continued. "Patsy's parents came in from Greensboro on Friday. Back then hospital rules were different. Visiting hours were very limited and strictly enforced. Since her parents and I couldn't stay with Patsy, we decided to go to the races that weekend."

The waiter brought their salads and inquired if they wanted fresh drinks. They declined.

"That Sunday," Dean said, "while Patsy dozed and I wolfed down hot dogs at the track with her folks, someone took Gina from the hospital nursery." He picked up his glass and finished off the drink. "We never saw her again."

Jake didn't mouth the obvious platitudes, and for that Patsy was grateful. "The theft of a newborn baby must have made headlines," he observed as he picked up his fork.

"It did," Dean said, "in Tennessee and much of the South, but those were the days before the Internet, before Web sites and blogs."

"The story might have had legs," Patsy added, "except that a few days later there was a big plane crash where hundreds of people were killed. That story dominated national head-lines for weeks. The media completely forgot about one little baby girl who had gone missing from a hospital in Nashville."

Jake buttered a piece of roll. "Kidnapping is a federal offense. Who investigated the crime?"

"The local police did initially," Dean answered, "but it didn't take them long to call in the FBI. They interviewed everybody who was even remotely connected with the hospital, people whose names appeared on patient logs, their families and friends, vendors and contractors, dozens of people."

"Sometimes more than once," Patsy noted.

"Babies are usually stolen by women," Jake remarked after the waitress had removed their salad plates and left.

Dean nodded. "So we learned. The nursing staff came under particularly intense scrutiny."

"There weren't many male nurses back then," Patsy added.

"Women undergoing fertility treatments and mothers of recently deceased or stillborn infants were questioned." Dean shook his head. "They turned up no one."

"Three days after Gina disappeared," Patsy said, "I was released from the hospital and allowed to take Kent home to our tiny apartment."

She remembered how crushed with guilt Dean had been for going to the track and not keeping watch over his tiny daughter, though he wouldn't have been allowed to stay with her in the nursery even if he had hung around the hospital.

"I stopped racing for the rest of that season," he said. "Thanks to financial help from Patsy's dad, I was able to spend my time with Patsy and Kent, but I drove the poor FBI agent in charge of the case crazy with my constant calls, questions, giving him what I thought might be leads." Dean emitted a half chuckle. "I still remember his name. Leman Cranston. Everybody called him Lamont after the radio series *The Shadow.* He was a family man himself, and he was patient with me, but he was operating in the dark, too. He did his best. It just wasn't enough."

Their main courses were served. Thick steaks for Dean and Jake. Grilled chicken breast with pineapple-mango chutney for Patsy.

"We concentrated all our attention on Kent," she said after sampling her chicken.

"What else could we do?" Dean asked. "We never left him alone."

Patsy shook her head. "We were afraid to turn our backs on him for a single second, afraid he, too, would disappear."

They ate in silence for several minutes. Patsy realized Jake had spoken very little. He'd let Dean and her ramble on undeterred. A good listener. No wonder he was so successful at what he did.

"Three months went by," Dean said after polishing off half his steak.

Three months of worry and desperate love, Patsy reflected. "Then we received word that the Mexican police had broken up a baby-smuggling ring. Apparently—" she put down her knife and fork "—they kidnapped and sold infants and babies to exclusive agencies who offered them for private adoption to wealthy couples, mostly in the Unites States."

Jake nodded and continued to eat.

"One of the women the Mexican police arrested described an infant who had reportedly been stolen from the States," Patsy went on, "a baby that perfectly matched Gina's description."

"Unfortunately the baby had died or was killed a week before the raid was conducted," Dean added, pushing back his plate, "and the body disposed of. It was never found. Of course, there was no DNA testing in those days, so even if the authorities had been able to recover the remains, they probably wouldn't have been able to positively identify it as Gina."

"But all the other information pretty well confirmed it was her," Patsy said. "A little girl of the right age with brilliant blue eyes and an unusually thick head of blond hair. Gina had blue eyes. Yes, I know, a lot of infants do at birth, then the color changes as they get older, but Gina also had the most incredible mop of yellow hair when she was born that anybody had ever seen. All the nurses commented on it, even the doctor."

"The documents the Mexican authorities were able to recover," Dean added, "confirmed the child's dimensions, weight, coloring, even her blood type."

Jake took it all in as he plunged into his baked potato, but said nothing.

Patsy remembered the ache in her heart, an ache that had never gone away. Their baby was dead. Everybody agreed. Dean fought it for a time but eventually came to accept it. Patsy said she did, too, but she didn't really. She couldn't. Deep down inside she harbored the unreasonable, unrealistic hope that maybe, just maybe, her daughter had survived. Patsy had to live with the selfish, shameful hope that the dead baby in Mexico hadn't been Gina, after all, but some other grieving mother's child.

Their plates removed, coffee was served. Nobody wanted dessert.

"And now," Jake finally said, "three decades later somebody is telling you Gina didn't die."

Three decades later, Patsy reflected. *Three decades in which my hope almost died.* Tears rolled down her cheeks. Annoyed by them, she rubbed them away with her napkin.

"What exactly do you want me to do?" Jake asked.

"Find out if it's true," Patsy said. "Find Gina."

CHAPTER FIFTEEN

ALL NIGHT LONG Adam puzzled and seethed over the telephone call from Dean. Tara had insisted she was writing a book about legends in NASCAR, that she wanted to give a human face to the people who made it one of the most popular sports in the country, that her goal was to be upbeat and positive. Sounded noble! But...

Belinda Goddard had told him more or less the same thing, and in fact, the article she wrote after the interview had been highly complimentary—a Trojan horse, he was later to realize.

Where was Tara coming from? Her obsession with Trey's flights to Mexico, her accusation that he might be running drugs, all suggested sensationalism rather than inspiration. She was willing to eavesdrop on private conversations and use snippets of them to jump to unfavorable conclusions, even when he gave her a perfectly feasible explanation. Clearly she wasn't out for a positive story. She wanted an exposé. The fact that Trey's night flights to Mexico were a matter of public record—what she would say was *in the public domain*—and were, therefore, a clear indication that he wasn't trying to hide anything, just maintain his privacy, didn't fit her agenda, so she set up a straw man, an accusation to be denied. The technique had destroyed Brent's racing career. Was Tara about to destroy Trey's—and in the process destroy Sanford Racing?

Now this tragedy of the Grossos! How much lower could a person go than to exploit the loss of a baby?

And yet…

He thought about the other two books Tara had written. *Hoops and Happiness* was about a bunch of disadvantaged kids who used sports, in this case basketball, not only to corral their teenage energies, but to learn and practice playing by the rules. Not a single one of the kids featured in the book went on to become NBA stars, though a couple of them did earn athletic scholarships for college. The point of the book wasn't how good they were at sports, but how good sports were for them. Practice didn't always make perfect, but it made a person better.

Rolling Uphill had been even more upbeat and inspirational. Tara could have focused on the tragic accident that had put promising young track star Daniel Wallingford in a wheelchair for the rest of his life. She could have played up the injustice of it all, how Danny's life had been ruined; she could have listed all the things he would no longer be able to do, complained about how unjust it was that the culprit in the car crash paid no significant price for his recklessness.

She chose, instead, to underscore the positive aspects in the boy's story, his determination to keep going, to excel at whatever he could do. She didn't ignore his agony in those last few hours of moving forward, muscle-aching wheel revolution by wheel revolution. But she placed emphasis on the culmination of his indomitable effort, on his triumph in reaching the top of the mountain and the view he could see from there.

Adam was out of bed before sunrise. He pictured Tara curled up in hers and had to restrain himself from calling her until after eight. By then he'd consumed four large mugs of strong coffee and was buzzed.

He dialed her number. She picked up on the second ring, sounding completely wide awake.

"What are you doing up so early?" he asked.

"It's not early. I've been up for hours, working on my book."

"I received a call last evening from Dean Grosso."

"Thanks for arranging for the interview, Adam. It went really well. I appreciate your help in setting it up."

"He told me you dropped a bombshell on them by bringing up their dead daughter."

"What? He told you…" Words seemed to fail her.

Adam didn't like that response. It sounded as if she'd brought up the subject but expected them to keep it quiet. "Did you?"

"No, I didn't!" she snapped, but only after a moment of hesitation. "Not to him."

"But you do know about Gina?" This wasn't the answer he'd been expecting.

"I found out about her when I was researching the Grossos."

"And you asked them about her? You're going to use a dead baby in your book? Oh, Tara. At Halesboro, when Dean and I talked, he said he was reconsidering his judgment of Brent based on what Alan had announced at the banquet. In light of that, I asked him for a favor—to give you the interview you wanted so badly. Now he calls me to complain that you went to his house and asked questions about a child they lost years ago, a nightmare they obviously don't want discussed in public."

"It wasn't like that."

"If you didn't ask questions about Gina, why would Dean say you did?"

"Adam, listen to me—"

"I am listening, and none of this makes any sense to me. Help me understand."

There was a long pause.

"Tara?"

"Oh, the hell with you. You're determined to think the worst of me."

"That's not true." But she had already disconnected.

Adam put down the phone and stared off into the middle distance. Why was she so upset? Because she had brought up the subject of Gina and was ashamed of it? Because she'd abused his trust by blindsiding Dean and Patsy into talking about a very painful subject?

He dialed her number again. The phone rang, but she didn't pick up, and neither did voice-mail. Apparently she wasn't interested in hearing from him or talking to him. Why was she so angry at him?

He'd give her time to calm down. He was planning to go into Charlotte later that afternoon. He'd stop by her place then and talk with her.

TARA WAS CONFUSED and angry as she put down the phone. She told herself she was angry at Adam for thinking she'd use a tragedy like a kidnapped infant as a draw for her book, but she was really angry with herself, because it was true. Not in the callous way he seemed to think, but did it really make any difference? Yes, motives counted.

She was about to call him back when the phone rang. Caller ID said unknown, but it had to be Adam. She let it ring and paced the floor for several minutes before finally deciding what to do. She wasn't going to allow him to define her or her work. Grabbing her purse and keys, she headed for the door.

The number he had called from wasn't his cell phone or the garage. She assumed, therefore, it was his unlisted home number. She'd feel like a fool if she showed up at the Lake Norman estate and he wasn't there, but she had little choice. She'd worry about how she would get through the front gate later. As a last resort, she'd call Kath and ask her to let her in, though she would prefer not to involve his mother in their dispute.

The gate was indeed closed. Tara drove past it, sure she'd find a service entrance. She did. It was open. She drove through, uncertain where she was headed or who she might encounter. Just as the roof of the main house came into view, she saw a smaller, single-story cottage in a copse below it. That had to be the guest house, where Adam lived. She took the short driveway to it. His SUV was parked under the double-wide carport.

She strode to the back door and knocked hard. Failing to receive an immediate response, she knocked harder. She was about to pound a third time when the door flew open, and he was towering over her. How could she have forgotten how handsome he was? He was wearing a fine-knit, light blue sweater and fawn-colored slacks.

"Tara." His voice was seductively low.

"We need to talk," she declared. "May I come in, or do you want me to catch my death out here in the cold?"

He arched his eyebrows in bafflement—though for the tiniest fraction of a second she was sure she glimpsed amusement twitching the corners of his mouth—then he took a step back by way of inviting her in.

She entered a small but neat and well-designed kitchen. The stainless-steel appliances gleamed. She didn't stop. There was another doorway directly in front of her. She marched through it into a living room, spun around and faced him.

"For someone who is so uptight about other people making judgments on scant evidence or jumping to conclusions, you do a pretty damn good job of it yourself."

"I wasn't aware I'd made any judgment. If you're refer-ring to your session with the Grossos, the evidence is incon-clusive. I was asking for an explanation. At least, I thought I was. Sit down." He motioned to the couch behind her.

"I'll stand." She wanted desperately to sit, afraid her shaky legs would give out from under her if she didn't, but she was determined not to let him dictate what she was going to do or say. "You accused me of bringing up the subject of Gina to Dean and Patsy."

Doubt darkened his features. "Didn't you?"

"No."

That stopped him for a moment. His forehead furrowed in confusion. "Are you saying Dean made it all up? Why would he lie about something like that? And how would he know you were interested in Gina if you didn't tell him?"

"I didn't hear what he said, so I don't know if it was accurate, or if the way you're reporting it is, for that matter. Either way, I'm not accusing him of lying. It's more likely you misinterpreted what he said. You heard what you wanted to hear, which is the worst about me."

She should be gratified by the hurt expression in his eyes, but she wasn't. This was coming out all wrong. Why was she trying to pick a fight with him? Guilty conscience, of course. He had a right to be upset with her for taking advantage of his generosity in getting her the interview.

"Maybe we both ought to sit down," she told him, "and I'll tell you what really happened."

She dropped onto the couch, folded her arms defensively and waited. He took the wing chair opposite her and crossed his legs as if he were at ease. She knew him well enough to recognize that he wasn't.

"I explained to you," she maintained, "that I was writing a book about NASCAR people."

"What's the title of this book, anyway?" he asked. "You never said."

"*Scandals and Secrets.*"

He crooked an eyebrow and mumbled a repetition of the title. "I can see why you didn't. The title itself reeks of tabloid journalism. *Scandals and Secrets,*" he scoffed. "It completely contradicts the spiel you gave me on this great piece of in-spirational literature you were writing."

"No, it doesn't," she shot back heatedly. "And I never said I was writing great literature. One of its themes, its major theme, in fact, is how NASCAR people overcome adversity. For example, your brother Brent was involved in a serious scandal that resulted in his leaving NASCAR altogether, but it hasn't crushed him. He's a successful charter-service owner and pilot, and he has continued in his own quiet way to pursue ex-oneration of the charges against him. I'm convinced he'll succeed."

Adam nodded appreciatively.

"And the Grossos have a secret," Tara continued. "When I went to their farm, I had to wait a few minutes before they were available. Not sure how I should approach the subject of Gina with them, I asked Juliana and Milo for their advice. Juliana became very upset and ordered me not to talk about Gina with Patsy and Dean. She was so agitated in her insistence that she worried me."

Tara looked Adam straight in the eyes. "So I didn't so much as even mention Gina's name," she declared. "We talked about Dean's past career, about Kent's move to Cargill-Grosso and about the team's future."

"So how did Dean know about your...foiled agenda?"

She was tempted to react to his choice of words but decided not to take the bait. "I don't know. Why don't you ask Dean? My guess is that Juliana or Milo told him."

Adam narrowed his eyes skeptically. "If the old folks were so adamant that you not mention Gina's name, why would they bring it up?"

"I have no idea, but obviously they did. They're also family. I'm not. That gives them rights I don't have and wouldn't presume to have."

Adam sat motionless for a minute, his back straight, then

he rubbed his jaw and let out a breath. "I owe you an apology. Thinking back on what Dean said, I realize you're right. I probably jumped to a conclusion he didn't intend." He lowered his gaze. "I should have known better."

She rose to her feet. "I'm glad we've gotten that settled. Apology accepted." She started across the room the way she'd come.

"Wait." He sprang to his feet and stood before her. "Don't go."

"There's not much point in my staying." Her tone was businesslike. "I'm happy we've been able to rectify this misunderstanding, but it's clear you don't trust me."

"Now who's jumping to conclusions?" he asked lightly, a smile on his lips. He appeared about to fold her in his arms, and she desperately wanted him to—but not yet. They had more to talk about, and now was the time for it.

"But you do distrust me," she said. "I'd like to know why."

He led her back to the sofa, sat beside her and took her hand. She wanted to resist, wanted to have the emotional strength to pull out of his grasp, but the warmth of his touch made her relent.

"Not you as a woman, Tara, but as a journalist. It's wrong of me to judge an entire profession based on the actions of a few, but my negative experience is hard to overcome."

"What experience is that?"

"Ashley."

"Your ex-wife?" Tara knew what the media reported, what the blogs discussed ad nauseam.

He nodded sadly. "I suppose, deep inside, I had reservations about her from the start. We weren't really suited."

"Because she was an airhead?"

He snorted. "Don't believe everything you read. Ashley was not stupid. I'll admit she wasn't all that intellectually curious, but she did have a master's degree in secondary education."

"She was a schoolteacher?" The press hadn't mentioned

that. Ashley Matenko's father was an oral surgeon, her mother his office manager. While in college, Ashley had been a clothing catalogue model, but there had been no mention of her master's degree.

"No," Adam said. "She never applied for a teaching certificate or even taught as a substitute. The thing is, she didn't do much of anything. She was a good tennis player and she'd been on the university swim team."

She certainly had the body for it, Tara reflected, based on the pictures of her she'd seen on the Internet.

"She wasn't a reader, for example," Adam went on. "She preferred to watch movies, go to plays and concerts. She tried out for a bit part in a local little theater production once—and I have to admit she was pretty good, but not great. I had the impression she wasn't trying hard enough to be a star. I will say this. She had a green thumb with houseplants."

Overall, Adam's ex-wife sounded rather shallow and dull and maybe that was the point. Tara was about to ask what he had seen in her, when he added, "Mostly she was beautiful. I don't think I ever met a woman with more poise and grace, and it was completely natural, not practiced or affected." He chuckled. "She was woman!"

Tara should have been insulted. He was praising the beauty and charm of another woman, his ex-wife no less, in a way that almost contrasted with Tara herself. Yet she didn't take offense. In a strange way, Adam was saying those external qualities weren't as important as substance. Or was she being naive, hung up on a guy who was drop-dead handsome but wasn't all that *suitable?* And what did this have to do with trust? Unless Ashley had been unfaithful. The media hadn't mentioned that, either. Just the opposite.

"After a couple of years of marriage," Adam went on, "when she told me she still wasn't ready to have children, I realized I'd made a mistake and asked for a divorce. She agreed without much of a fight. Everything might have gone through quickly and relatively painlessly, if it hadn't been for Belinda."

"Who's Belinda?"

"Belinda Goddard was Ashley's best friend, a freelance journalist."

Tara felt a knot form in her stomach. She recognized the name. Goddard was a muckraker of the most vicious kind. She was currently working for a national tabloid, but rumors had been circulating for months that she was getting her own TV talk show.

"Belinda had asked me for a personal interview soon after Ashley introduced us," Adam continued. "She'd been just starting out then with a local newspaper, didn't have the reputation she has now. It probably won't surprise you to hear that I turned her down. I would have been willing to talk about the team, but she wanted to talk about me. I didn't see any point."

He was right, Tara reflected. She wasn't surprised.

"So Belinda went to Ashley and Ashley convinced me to grant her the interview. This was several months before I asked for a divorce. I agreed to meet Belinda one afternoon at a fancy restaurant where she was scheduled to have lunch with a local celebrity—or said she was. As it turned out the celebrity had stood her up, and that day I was running behind and arrived at the restaurant twenty minutes late. To make amends for her having to sit there by herself for so long, I persuaded the owner to keep the kitchen open a little longer for us. Belinda said she would like to have a glass of wine with lunch, so I ordered one of the more expensive labels on the list. She asked me questions, and I tried to answer them in terms of the team. Finally it was time for us to leave. She had come to the restaurant by taxi, so I offered to drive her home."

Tara thought she could see what was coming, but she let him tell it.

"She invited me inside, saying she had a few more questions to ask for her article. I waited in the living room while she went to freshen up. She came out of her bedroom wearing this thin, diaphanous thing. I'm sure I stared."

"And she came on to you."

"Pretty obvious, isn't it? Before I had a chance to escape, she positioned herself between me and the door and just stood there. I didn't touch her, but I am a man and I responded the way a man does and, well, she touched me."

He closed his eyes for a minute and took a deep breath.

"I walked around her and left. Nothing more happened. Belinda wrote a very complimentary article about me, so I dismissed the incident as the result of her having had too much wine—she'd drunk most of the bottle—and not eating enough. I tried to put it out of my mind."

"Until the divorce," Tara prompted.

"Until the divorce," he confirmed unhappily. "Ashley accused me of infidelity. I was stunned. I'd never been unfaithful to her. I saw firsthand the kind of pain my father caused my mother, and I resolved not to be like him. When I was small, my mother used to laugh, but in those last years of my father's life she stopped. He's been gone almost fifteen years now, but she still doesn't laugh, not the way she used to."

"I'm sorry," Tara said.

A moment passed. "We were talking about Ashley and Belinda. In court Ashley's attorney asked me questions such as had I ever seen Belinda without her clothes on, had she ever touched me…well, you get the idea. I could have lied, of course, but I'd taken an oath. I also couldn't be sure Belinda hadn't had hidden cameras in her apartment. Getting caught in a lie would have made it worse. Remember what the security cameras in that bar did to Brent. In his case he honestly didn't remember ever meeting Mike Jones until the tape proved he had. On the other hand, I could hardly contend I didn't remember seeing Belinda take her clothes off in front of me. So Ashley's lawyer was able to use my own words against me, make me out to be no better than my father. My protests that it hadn't happened the way it was being portrayed fell on deaf ears. After all, Belinda had written favorably about me. We'd continued to be friends in public and private, and so on."

"So Ashley set you up?" Tara concluded. "She must have seen a divorce on the horizon."

"She denied it," Adam said. "She claimed it was all Belinda's idea, that she'd had designs on me from the beginning. When she made her move and I rejected her, she decided to take her revenge and help Ashley at the same time."

"A woman scorned."

He nodded. "I guess. What I do know is that with her access to the media and the evidence she'd trumped up, my reputation was trashed, my integrity questioned, and Ashley ended up with a fifty-million-dollar judgment, instead of the two million we'd previously agreed on."

"How did that happen?" Tara asked.

"On the stand Belinda claimed I'd told her that I was holding out on Ashley financially. It wasn't true. Besides, if I'd been hiding money, I'd hardly have told her. What was true, however, was that I had money in a separate account, money I'd earned before our marriage to which Ashley had no legal right. The judge didn't care. There had been activity in the account after we were married, therefore, she declared that that made it community property, and she awarded half of it to Ashley."

"That's ridiculous."

"I fought it and eventually got it reduced, but it still cost

me. The irony of all this is that Ashley and I might have separated as friends, had it not been for Belinda."

"So that's why you distrust journalists and, by extension,
me."

"I was wrong about you."

Tara left a few minutes later. Adam had tried to coax her
to stay. He repeated his apology. She thanked him for it but
refused to hang around. She needed to think, and she couldn't
do that in his presence.

She drove home slowly, sat in her living room, forgot to
eat and got nothing at all accomplished on her book.

That evening, she called her mother. Shirley could play the
blowsy bleach blonde or the charming guest, but at heart she
was a mom with a good deal of maternal and womanly
wisdom.

Tara brought her up-to-date, concluding with her confron-
tation with Adam.

"I had no idea about the Grosso kidnapping," Shirley said.
"Heartbreaking story. I wonder how I would have ever
survived if something had happened to you."

Tara thought about the Grossos, how badly she'd handled
the situation and how it must look to Adam. Yes, she'd given
him reason to be distrustful.

"What should I do about Adam?" she finally asked her
mother.

"How do you feel about him?"

Tara paused. "I think I love him, Mom."

"Then give him a reason to trust you."

"How?" Tara asked.

"I'll have to leave that to you to figure out, honey."

CHAPTER SIXTEEN

JAKE MCMASTERS reviewed the notes he'd made at his dinner with Dean and Patsy. An intriguing case—three decades old. Now, all of a sudden, there was a rumor that the victim was not only alive and well, but that she was in some way connected to the NASCAR community.

An Internet search listed numerous Web sites dealing with missing and exploited children. By using the keywords *Gina Grosso*, he was able to hone in on the blog that had recently discussed her. Jake searched the web for newspaper accounts of the kidnapping, but the story was too old for most papers to have digitized their files that went that far back. A review of the meticulously kept scrapbook Patsy had given him, however, had saved him innumerable hours of manual research through dusty archives.

Finally Jake did a people search for Leman Cranston. He found the retired FBI special agent living with his grandson's family on a farm in West Virginia. The drive there was slow through the mountains but beautiful, even in winter.

"Yeah, they used to call me Lamont Cranston." The seventy-seven-year-old chuckled. They were in the living room of a log house, sitting in front of a stone fireplace where a crackling fire radiated cheerful warmth. "Not many people around anymore who remember the old radio-mystery series. So I'm back to being called Lee or Leman. Yeah, I remember the Grosso kidnapping. Sad. Two young parents. Kids really.

Had twins, a boy and a girl. Somebody stole the little girl." He tipped back his mug of dark beer. "Never did find her."

"What about that Mexican baby-smuggling ring? Think they were involved?" Jake asked.

"Everybody thought so, but I wasn't so sure. Somehow it didn't feel right, seemed too easy, too pat."

"You have an alternative theory?"

The retired lawman scratched his chin. "You've been in this business a while, Jake. You know how it is when you get a feeling that things don't quite fit, but you don't know why. Situations where you have suspicions about certain people but can't rationally justify them. I always had the feeling this was a local job, that taking that little girl was something personal—"

"Personal? Against the parents?"

Leman shook his head. "Nah. Those kids didn't have any enemies. The father, Dean, was competitive, sure, but that was a different matter. What I mean is that the person who took the baby did it for personal reasons, wasn't part of a syndicate or crime ring. I still think that, though I can't tell you why any better today than I could back then."

"Did you have anyone specific in mind?"

"Nope, and that was the most frustrating part of the case, like chasing a shadow, if you'll excuse the pun. Usually you've got a prime suspect, or at least someone of interest you don't feel right about, but I didn't in that case. Like I said, frustrating."

"Man or woman?"

"Oh, a woman. Definitely. That much I'm sure of." He paused. "Sorry I can't be more specific. If I had more, believe me, I would have followed up on it. I've thought about that kidnapping over the years. Nothing more satisfying than solving a case involving children, and nothing more heart-wrenching than having to break the news to parents that their kid is dead."

Jake left the former FBI agent and returned to North

Carolina. Back in his office he called a friend in Monterrey, Mexico. Jake and Savio Estaban had worked a number of international investigations together.

Jake passed on what he knew about the abduction.

"Records back then were handwritten," Savio told him, "and not always very carefully. I'll see if I can find anything, but I'm not making any promises."

"What I'm particularly interested in," Jake explained, "is whether they ever found the remains of the baby they claimed was Gina Grosso. I know it's a long shot, but if there's any possibility those remains still exist, we might be able to do a DNA match. If they are Gina's, we can at least bring closure for the family. If the remains are not hers, the door is still wide open, and my work has only begun."

After he hung up, Jake continued to review the information before him. The question that kept niggling was why this subject was coming up now. It had been three decades since the Grossos' infant daughter was stolen, three decades since baby Gina reportedly died. Jake could find no further public mention of the incident once the big airplane crash had knocked the story off the front page. Yet all of a sudden, the name Gina Grosso popped up again. Why?

Was it possible Gina Grosso herself had only recently become aware of her true identity? If that was so, why hadn't she simply come forward? If someone else had only just discovered her identity, why hadn't that person gone to her and resolved the matter? Why all the mystery? Why this cruel game of cat and mouse?

That brought Jake to the question of the author of the blog entries. Who was it? He had learned his way around the Internet over the years. Maybe he wasn't a digital genius, but he had become something of an expert on search engines and how to identify senders. He also knew that if someone really wanted to stay hidden, they could, which seemed to be the case here.

Could Tara Dalton herself be the originator of the blog entry? Was it possible that in researching the Grosso family, she'd learned of their missing baby and was now stirring things up in order to make her new book more marketable?

He conducted a preliminary search on Tara Dalton. No federal record. He checked her name in North Carolina and the neighboring states. No police records there, either, except for a parking ticket in Atlanta a couple of years ago and a speeding ticket on I-30 a year before that.

He checked her parents. Both honest, upstanding citizens. Her sister, Emma-Lee, was clean. Her other sister, Mallory, was a television star and a beauty queen. No scandals in her life—so far. None of which proved Tara was innocent, of course, but the likelihood of someone with a previously spotless reputation suddenly taking it south didn't seem likely.

Her first book, *Hoops and Happiness,* had apparently sold well without any marketing tricks, and her second, *Rolling Uphill,* had made it to the bestseller list, also without any promotional gimmicks. Why would she suddenly sink to such despicable tactics?

A naturally suspicious man, Jake entertained yet another possibility, that *she* was Gina. Looking at her picture, the conjecture didn't seem completely without merit. Tara had an oval face very much like Patsy's and the slightest hint of a cleft in her chin that she might have inherited from Dean.

If she was Gina Grosso, how had she learned of her secret identity? How long had she known it? And why hadn't she simply presented herself to the family? The blogger said Gina was involved with NASCAR. Writing a book about it and being a close friend of an owner qualified.

The main reason for anyone coming forward and claiming to be the Grossos' long-lost daughter was obvious. Money. Plenty of it.

At present Dean and Patsy had two children, two direct heirs. Kent and his younger sister, Sophia. They would inherit not just from their parents, but no doubt from their great-grandparents. Jake didn't know how much was involved, but he had no doubt the combined estates ran to the tens of millions of dollars, maybe the hundreds. Even if the family assets were split three ways, instead of two, the individual shares would still be substantial and the difference hardly missed by Kent or Sophia. Kent was a NASCAR driver, earning millions of dollars a year. Sophia was engaged to Justin Murphy, another NASCAR driver who earned at least as much and was in line to receive a substantial amount from his uncle Hugo. Jake had learned a long time ago, however, that wealth wasn't about how much it would buy but how much power it could wield.

The question remained. Why? If she was the real Gina Grosso or even a pretender, why had Tara not gone directly to the family to stake her claim?

Sometimes you have to look people in the eye to decide for yourself if you believe them.

Time to visit Tara.

TARA KEPT THINKING of her mother's advice. *Give him a reason to trust you.* Like what? About the only thing that would make him trust her under the circumstances would be if she gave up writing the book altogether, but that would be doubly foolish, a lose-lose situation for her. She would lose the book she had contracted to do, and for which she'd already received a partial advance, and she wouldn't really gain his trust; the next time something happened that disturbed him, he'd expect her to be the one to concede. Not a chance.

Okay, then, the book project would continue, but she'd have to ensure nothing she wrote hurt innocent people. The easiest way to accomplish that, of course, would be to simply ignore the subject of Gina Grosso. Yet the story of a missing child, one kidnapped and maybe murdered, was a compelling mystery, one she was certain would tug at the hearts of her readers. The potential for a happy ending—if Gina was still alive and well—was even more compelling.

She turned on her laptop and went to the blog site to reread the entries about Gina Grosso. No new information, just groundless speculations about who she might be and where she might work.

Tara was about to type in a new entry, pose another question to the original blogger, when the doorbell rang.

Could it be Adam? If it was, she didn't want him to see she was visiting this Web site. It had stirred up enough trouble between them already. She shut down the computer and went to answer the door.

She'd never seen the man facing her. He wasn't quite as tall as Adam and was probably in his late forties, a big man, leaning on a cane. He didn't smile as he introduced himself.

"Ms. Dalton, my name is Jake McMasters. I'm a private investigator looking into your claim that Gina Grosso, the twin sister of Kent Grosso, is still alive." He removed a business card from his inside coat pocket and handed it to her. "I'm wondering if you would be willing to discuss the matter with me. Confidentially, of course."

"It's not *my* claim. I'm just repeating what I read on a blog." She examined the card he'd handed her. It confirmed his name and occupation, but anybody could have a business card made up.

As if reading her mind, he said, "If you would like to call Dean or Patsy Grosso to verify who I am, I'll be glad to wait here. If you don't want to invite me in, I fully understand. Perhaps we can meet somewhere public. Just tell me where and when."

It wasn't wise to invite a complete stranger into her apartment, and she knew appearances could be deceiving. The cane he was carrying, for example—did he need it because of an infirmity or was it a weapon? Just because he looked trustworthy and harmless didn't mean he was. On the other hand, this was her turf, she wasn't defenseless, and her instincts told her to take a chance.

"Please come in." She stepped aside to let him pass.

When he left an hour later, again leaning heavily on his cane, Tara doubted she'd told Jake McMasters anything he didn't already know. She'd explained how she'd come upon the information about Gina and given him the Web site addresses of the blog where an anonymous source said Gina was still alive. He'd seemed a bit surprised that she was willing to share her sources, but what was the point of holding out? They were all easy enough to find, and she really did want to help the Grossos resolve the question of their child's fate.

She returned to her laptop and booted it up. Her search engine sent her a pop-up. She clicked on it. Not Gina or any of the Grossos.

Trey Sanford.

She followed the links to the blog that had first reported Trey's midnight trips out of a remote airstrip. The same blogger, who apparently had some sort of crush on the youngest Sanford brother, reported that Trey had been seen coming out of Santa Ysidra Hospital in Monterrey, Mexico, with a very lovely senorita wearing a nurse's uniform. They were both laughing.

Tara couldn't keep from smiling. Her first instinct was now confirmed.

It only took a minute for Tara to learn that Santa Ysidra Hospital was primarily a charity hospital for children with neurological disorders.

A series of questions ran through Tara's mind. What was

Trey doing at a children's hospital? Was his only interest there the nurse he'd been seen with? What was the nature of their relationship? Friends? Lovers? Could she be his wife? If so, why was Trey keeping the marriage secret? How did the supplies Trey had talked to Adam about play into any of this? If Trey was helping support the hospital, why not make it known so he could raise more funds? Was it possible he had a child there?

THE NIGHT WAS as restless as any Adam had experienced in a long time. He couldn't stop thinking about Tara, about the time they'd spent together, about how she had charged into his house, determined to set the record straight, to exonerate herself in his eyes for the chaos she'd sewn at the Grossos'. The trouble she'd caused hadn't been intentional. He realized that now, but why couldn't she just stay out of other people's business? What Dean and Patsy had endured when they'd lost their daughter was bad enough. To dredge it all up after so many years was inexcusable.

In spite of everything, he was hungry this morning. He hadn't eaten last night, and his stomach was now grumbling to remind him. Since it was still early, he knew his mother wouldn't have eaten yet, so he got dressed and trekked up to the house. Larine would happily fix a platter of flapjacks for the two of them.

Kath was already in the kitchen, pouring herself a cup of coffee, when he arrived.

"Good," she said to him. "I'm glad you're here. I'm in the mood for pancakes and sausage and always feel bad when I ask Larine to fix them just for me."

Adam chuckled. "I saw her pulling into the driveway as I was walking over."

A moment later the housekeeper entered the back door and greeted them. Larine had worked for Kath for more than twenty years, knew all the family's secrets and kept them to herself. She handed Kath the morning paper, rolled up in its usual plastic sleeve.

After hanging up her wool coat, Larine asked, "Bacon or sausage with the flapjacks?"

Adam winked at his mother and poured Larine a big mug of coffee. "Sausage."

"Adam, look at this," his mother said to him, as she stared at the newspaper headlines.

"What?"

Kath passed the first section to him. "'Search on for Grossos' Missing Daughter.'"

He felt his heartbeat stammer as he picked up the paper. The story was there. All of it. That Patsy Grosso had given birth to twins in Nashville. That Kent had a twin sister by the name of Gina, who had been stolen from the hospital a few days after her birth and never seen again. That she was believed to have died in Mexico soon after being kidnapped.

Adam's heart sank. The Grossos didn't deserve to have their private agony plastered all over the papers. Then he read the paragraph that really provoked his ire. "Sources close to the Grossos have disclosed exclusively to this paper that Tara Dalton, best-selling author of sports biographies *Hoops and Happiness* and *Rolling Uphill,* is currently writing a book about the famous NASCAR family. She reportedly recently uncovered information that suggests Gina Grosso may not have died at all but is currently involved with NASCAR, just like her famous father and brother."

CHAPTER SEVENTEEN

ADAM WISHED NOW that he hadn't asked for pancakes for breakfast. He didn't want to offend Larine or upset his mother by turning down a second stack, but they seemed to be sitting like stones in his belly. The coffee was hot; he used it to wash them down. He was about to decline a third batch when Brent entered the room.

"I didn't know you were here," Adam remarked at his entrance.

"Got in late last night." He kissed his mother on the cheek. "Mmm. Pancakes." He gave Larine a peck, as well. "No one makes them better."

"Fix yourself a cup of coffee, Mr. Brent," she said, "and I'll have you a stack in a jiffy."

"You look like you just bit into a very sour lemon," Brent said to his brother. "What's up? I know it isn't Larine's cooking."

Adam pushed the newspaper, headlines up, toward his brother. "Have you seen this?"

Brent finished pouring his coffee and dragged the paper closer. After reading the article, he looked over at his brother. "It would appear your girlfriend is getting an early start on her PR campaign."

Adam bristled. "She didn't release that information."

"If you say so." Brent tilted his head. "So who did? I bet the reporter who wrote the story won't tell you. Nobody else has anything to gain by broadcasting this sensationalism."

"Because she has a book coming out about them?" Adam countered. "Come on. That's a stretch, don't you think? Her book won't be released for months. Publicity is one thing, but this seems to me much too far in advance." Was that the only reason he was defending her? Hadn't he said she'd do anything to achieve her goals? "The story will probably have petered out by then," he added. "Besides, it's not her style."

Brent looked at his mother, inviting her assessment. She only shrugged.

"I suppose I could be wrong," Brent opined offhandedly. "We talked for more than an hour, and to be fair, she didn't once ask an inappropriate, flippant or accusatory question, nor did I ever hear her make any statements that would suggest she had a bias or an agenda. But then, I imagine Belinda was just as nonthreatening when she did a job on you, too."

Adam fumed. He also resented the comparison, though he had to admit his brother was right—about Belinda. The woman had been cool and professional when she interviewed him. There'd never been a threat, just a one-two punch he should have seen coming. He'd been naive and trusting. He supposed that was what Brent was trying to alert him to now.

Brent doctored his coffee with cream and a half teaspoon of sugar. "From what I could tell, Tara was collecting information, nothing more, asking questions to get clarification. She certainly didn't appear to have an ax to grind." He sampled his coffee. "On the other hand, we haven't seen what she's written yet, either."

Larine placed a stack of pancakes in front of him.

"I'm sure everything will be fine." He slathered the flapjacks with butter. "In fact, I'll be very surprised if it turns out to be much different from the way she interviewed me." He poured the syrup. "Except—" he paused with a loaded fork halfway to his open mouth "—didn't you tell me she wasn't averse to a little blackmail to get what she wanted?"

"Blackmail?" Kath froze, clearly disturbed.

Adam huffed in frustration, scrunched up his face and threw his arm around the back of his stool. "When Tara and I first met," he explained to their mother, "she wanted to interview me. I said no, of course."

"Of course," Brent mumbled between generous bites.

"She asked if I was afraid to give an interview," Adam went on, "because she might ask me about Trey's secret trips to Mexico."

Tight lipped, Kath lowered her cup to the countertop.

"I gave her the interview," Adam went on. "I figured it would be better than having her speculate all over the place. Turned out she wasn't satisfied with just an interview. She wanted full access to Sanford Racing, and she made sure she got it by suggesting this time that Trey's clandestine night trips to Mexico were because he was running drugs."

Kath brought her fingers up to her mouth, her eyes wide. Brent stopped eating and lay his knife and fork on the edge of the plate. He looked at his older brother. "Was she serious?"

Adam shook his head. "She backed off the instant I called her on it," he admitted. "Claimed she didn't really believe it, but that was how it looked."

"You realize her true beliefs are immaterial," Brent observed. "The point is she was willing to use dirty tricks and innuendo to get what she wanted, and it worked. I think that newspaper article—" he pointed to the paper "—is just another example of how far she's willing to go. In this case, to get publicity for her upcoming book."

Brent grinned and resumed eating as Larine added another piping-hot stack of pancakes to his plate.

TARA TOOK ONE LOOK at the headlines and cringed. She wasn't just appalled by the reference to her in the article, she was infuriated by it. Her immediate impulse was to go down to the newspaper office and demand to know who gave the reporter the information about her, but she knew it wouldn't do any good. They would never reveal their source, and she didn't blame them, but she understood a little better how Adam and Brent must have felt when people were writing and commenting about them. In his case, what they were saying wasn't true, whereas in hers…

Who could have released that information? Certainly not the Grossos. No one else knew about her interest in Gina except Adam…and Jake McMasters.

But why would a private investigator go public? He'd made it clear he was carrying on a confidential investigation for Dean and Patsy. Why, then, reveal this very personal information?

Even as she was puzzling over that conundrum, however, her mind was preoccupied with yet another—how would Adam react when he saw the news item?

He'd given her the benefit of the doubt when Dean accused her of breaching a trust. Would he this time? Or would he assume, because her name was mentioned, that she was the source who'd committed the violation of privacy? He distrusted writers, and from what she'd learned about his divorce, he had good reason to. He and Brent had been the victims of misinformation, so he would understand that she was not accountable for what people reported.

She needed to talk to Adam, but she had to talk to Dean and Patsy, too, make them understand she wasn't the person responsible for this news leak. Maybe even before that, though, she ought to contact McMasters, find out if he knew what was going on. Perhaps this was part of some master—McMaster—plan. To what? Flush out Gina Grosso? Seemed like an awfully clumsy way to do it.

She located the card he'd given her and dialed the number. Voice mail immediately picked up. Her impulse was to let him know she was displeased with the situation, but that would only put him on the defensive and she might never get to talk to him.

In a calm voice she said, "Mr. McMasters, I need to speak with you as soon as possible about a matter of mutual interest. Thank you." She left her telephone number and disconnected.

Still holding the instrument, she started dialing the Grossos, but then reconsidered. If they blamed her for this violation of their privacy, whoever answered the phone—especially if it was Juliana—would probably hang up on her. Better to appear in person. She might be asked to leave, but like her appearing at Adam's door, her chances of being heard were better in face to face.

BREAKFAST WASN'T sitting well. Not the pancakes as much as the table talk, Adam thought as he drove. Brent had been stirring the pot, being a troublemaker. Nothing new about that, but Tara was driving him crazy. He didn't know what to make of his feelings for her. He didn't understand them, and he didn't trust them. He didn't want to think that she had intentionally leaked the story to the press, but could he be sure? He should be. He wanted to be.

Did he love her? He thought of his marriage. He'd told Ashley he loved her. He'd believed he did when he said it. He'd certainly been attracted to her. How could he not be? She was beautiful, charming, feminine. She'd made him feel good. She'd told him she loved him, and he still liked to think she'd meant it at the time, too, but they'd been wrong for each other. He'd trusted his heart, instead of his head, and it had led to heartache.

So how could he be certain about what he was feeling now about Tara? He didn't doubt their physical attraction. Maybe she didn't have the exceptional beauty of Ashley, or even her sister Mallory, but Tara had qualities that appealed to him even more—a genuine warmth, a unique personality—and she posed a constant challenge. She would never be boring, never be someone he would take for granted.

He pulled up behind her apartment house and took an empty visitor's slot. Tara's yellow car was in its accustomed place.

She answered his knock immediately.

"Adam." She looked more surprised, even disturbed, than pleased to see him. Guilty conscience? "I was just getting ready to go out. You can come in for a minute." She stepped back to admit him.

He wanted to take her in his arms, assure her everything was going to be all right. If she was the source of the article, she'd made a mistake, but it wasn't insurmountable. They'd get past it…but when he moved toward her, she backed away. He raised the paper he'd brought with him.

"Did you give the story about Gina Grosso to the press?" He asked the question as casually as he knew how.

She stared at him. "You think I did?"

"I'm simply asking, Tara. If—"

She let out a breath and turned away. "It wouldn't do any good to deny it, I suppose," she muttered, facing the window, her arms folded. "You wouldn't believe me."

He came up behind, put his hands gently on her shoulders. She shrugged them off. He stepped back. "I will, if you tell me you didn't."

She shook her head, her chin raised, as she continued to stare out at the bare trees. "But you have to ask."

"I'll take that as a no," he said. "Any idea who did?"

She spun around to face him. "Maybe you did, or Dean or Patsy."

He felt suddenly helpless. "Tara, sweetheart, calm down. Why are you so upset? You're not making any sense. You know how I feel about the press. I'd never go to them with a story like this. And why would Dean or Patsy leak it? That's crazy." He knew the words were a mistake the moment they left his mouth. He hadn't meant them literally. They were a figure of speech, but that wasn't how she heard them.

"Oh, crazy me," she snapped.

"Tara—"

"Maybe it was Jake McMasters, I don't know."

"Who's Jake McMasters?"

"The private investigator Dean and Patsy hired to try to find their daughter," she answered distractedly. "He was here yesterday. I gave him all the information I had, told him about the research I'd done, how I'd discovered Kent had had a twin sister. I gave him the Internet address of the blog where somebody claimed Gina is alive and connected with NASCAR."

"Why would a private investigator take it to the press? I thought they liked to work in the shadows."

She shrugged. "It's a new world. There are no secrets anymore, remember? Maybe the way investigators do things these days is to stir things up and see what settles."

Adam stared at her, not quite sure how serious she was or how to respond.

"Look," she finally said, breaking the silence between them, "you're not happy with the way things are going between us. I'm not, either." She paused, as if mulling over a decision. "I think it would be best if you and I didn't see each other for a while."

"Not see each other? What are you talking about?" He had a sinking feeling in the pit of his stomach. "And how long is a while?"

She squeezed her eyes closed for several seconds. He realized she was fighting tears. "Maybe forever." She sounded tired, worn-out, defeated. "I don't know. You don't have any respect for my profession. You're convinced I'd sell out my own mother for a story…or a headline."

"Tara, that's not true, and it's not fair. You can't—"

"We're not right for each other. You don't trust me. I understand why. You've been hurt, and I'm sorry about that, but I'm not the one who hurt you, and I'm tired of always having to prove myself to you."

He stared at her. "You can't be serious about our not seeing each other." He started toward her, his arms outstretched, but she backed away from him, her palms up, shielding herself from contact.

"Please go, Adam." She walked to the door and opened it, then stood back, her hand still on the knob.

"Tara…"

She held her chin up—did it quiver?—and waited for him to leave.

He blinked hard, realized his mouth was open, closed it, focused straight ahead and walked out.

She gave vent to the tears after he left. He didn't understand why she'd asked him to leave, why she'd ended the relationship between them. She wasn't sure she could fully explain it to herself, except that it wasn't just about him, about what he'd done, about how he had disappointed her. It was about her, too.

He was attracted to her as a woman, of that she had no doubt. She was certainly attracted to him. But he didn't trust her as a writer. She understood that. He and his family had been burned badly by the media in general, and by journalists in particular. The scars of those encounters hadn't yet healed, maybe they never would, but writing was in her blood as much as NASCAR was in his. She felt offended, insulted that he would put her in the same category with Belinda Goddard. Yet…

Tara had to acknowledge that in some ways she had acted just like the tabloid guttersnipe he abhorred—and Tara abhorred, too—tricking him into giving her an interview, then upping the ante by blackmailing him with a wild accusation for which she had only the flimsiest of circumstantial evidence.

She understood, too, his anger about the embarrassment and pain she'd caused the Grossos, how it had looked as if she were using a dead baby to get a sensational story. That her motivation was benevolent was immaterial. Her tactic of secrecy had been unworthy of a professional. More importantly, in adhering to it she had abused Adam's friendship. The decent thing would have been to tell him up front what her goals and objectives were, then give him the opportunity to decide whether he wanted to support her. She hadn't, she realized now, because she knew he wouldn't have, and she didn't want to be talked out of her grand plan.

She'd hoped he'd had more confidence in her.

She'd get over him. She had to. For her sanity's sake. For her heart's sake.

ADAM FELT he owed Dean and Patsy an apology for the pain the headlines about Gina must have brought then. He called ahead to make sure they would be home, then drove to Villa Grosso in Mooresville. Dean met him at the door and led him quietly to the den, where Patsy was sitting with an unopened magazine in her lap.

Dean offered the perfunctory drink, which Adam declined. They sat.

"I just want to tell you both in person how sorry I am about the newspaper article and for any part I might have played in facilitating—"

"It ticked me off, I can tell you that," Dean stated.

"Me, too," Patsy agreed, "until I started thinking about it. Then I realized it might be the best thing that could have happened."

Bewildered, Adam said, "I don't understand."

"I've never let myself believe my baby is dead," Patsy

explained. "This blogger Tara found says our daughter is still alive."

"It may not be true," Dean was quick to interject.

"I know that," his wife replied, head momentarily bowed. She looked up at Adam. "But now we have a chance to learn more about what happened. Maybe we'll be able to find Gina."

"Or at least put closure to this," Dean added. "I never wanted to believe she was dead, either, but the police insisted she was, and accepting that seemed to be the healthiest response. Patsy's right, though. It's hard to say goodbye to one of your children, even when you've only held her a few minutes."

"But you didn't leak the story to the newspaper?" Adam said.

"Certainly not," Dean replied curtly.

"I thought Tara had," Patsy contributed, "but we received flowers from her a little while ago with a handwritten card. She apologized for stirring things up but assured us she was not responsible for the story in the paper."

"Then who was?" Adam asked. "*Some*body did."

He received blank stares in response.

"I understand you have a private investigator looking into the matter," Adam ventured.

"My cousin," Patsy explained, "Jake McMasters."

"Can you give me his address?"

An hour later Adam was sitting in front of an unimpressive gunmetal-gray desk in an equally bland office building not far from downtown Charlotte.

"Dean called to say you were coming," the man behind the desk told him. "What can I do for you, Mr. Sanford?"

"First, I'd like to ask you a question." When Jake didn't respond, Adam went on, "Did you give the story about Gina to the newspaper?"

"I did not."

Adam studied the man's face. He didn't suppose someone in his profession would shy away from a bald-faced lie, and he suspected this particular man would be good at it, but Adam believed him. "Do you know who did?"

"I presumed Ms. Dalton."

"She denies it."

"And you believe her?"

"I do."

"Why?"

"Because I know her." *Because I love her.*

Again the man behind the desk lapsed into silence.

Finally Adam said, "Mr. McMasters, I'd like to hire you to find out who *did* leak the story to the newspaper."

CHAPTER EIGHTEEN

THE OFFICIAL NASCAR racing season always started in Daytona. Milo Grosso could—and frequently did—recount stories of the first NASCAR race when part of the track was actually run on the beach itself, when calculating the tide was part of a driver's racing strategy. Conditions had changed in the sixty years since then. Instead of fifteen thousand people standing around to watch whoever showed up with a car, the entry fee and the guts to race, the contest now was strictly controlled and the crowd numbered two hundred thousand, plus the millions watching it on TV. The weekend before the official start, however, was an exhibition race, a two-stage un-official nighttime competition that gave a glimpse of who to keep an eye on in the upcoming season. The race didn't count for points, but it carried a large purse and a good deal of prestige. Competitors were made up of all the pole starters from the previous season, plus former NASCAR Sprint Cup Series champions—in other words, NASCAR's best.

Tara knew all this. She'd grown up in NASCAR, and now, thanks to Adam, she'd met many of the participants, drivers, team members, owners and sponsors. But there was only one person who dominated her thoughts.

She'd spied him in the Sanford-garage area talking to Trey and his crew chief, Ethan Hunt, while various other team members busied themselves getting the No. 483 car ready for the opening competition. Adam apparently hadn't seen her.

At least that was the impression he'd given. Tara's parents wanted to rush over to him and say hello, but Tara convinced them that it wasn't a good idea, that he didn't need the interruption just then.

"I never thought I'd have to face this kind of dilemma," Shirley told Tara as they wove their way through the milling crowd toward the grandstand.

"What's that, Mom?" She was only half listening, her concentration divided. She loved being at the race, feeling the excitement, knowing Adam was never too far away, afraid of bumping into him face-to-face, afraid she'd miss him.

"Deciding who to root for, silly," her mother replied. "You know I've always been a Dean Grosso fan. When rumors began to spread last year that he would be retiring at the end of the season, I automatically figured I'd change my allegiance to his son. Kent's a fabulous driver, and when Juliana was so sweet to arrange for us to get these garage passes—" she held up the plastic-coated credentials at the end of a woven lanyard "—well…I feel like a traitor if I don't cheer for Kent."

"So what's the problem, Mom?" Tara asked as she continued to scan the crowd for familiar faces.

"Well, when you and Adam—"

"We've broken up, Mom. I told you that."

"Trey's our driver," Buddy contributed, hardly looking up from the program he was studying. "I bet he'll finish in the top five this year."

"Let's get to our seats," Mallory said. "We can see the race better from there."

TREY CAME IN SECOND in the first segment of the race, twenty laps, only three seconds behind the leader, Kent Grosso. In the ten-minute break that followed, teams were allowed to do anything to the car they would normally be permitted to do during a pit stop—fuel up, change tires and tire pressures, install wedges and make a variety of adjustments to the suspension that would improve handling on the track.

The second segment of the race was fifty laps, a distance calculated to necessitate a pit stop. The strategic challenge was determining when to take it: early, so it was behind the driver and he could concentrate on getting and staying ahead of the opposition; in the middle, after he'd had some time to evaluate the roadway and the mind-set of the other drivers; or later, after he'd spent most of the race running light and therefore presumably faster. Each option had its benefits and pitfalls.

"What's your plan?" Adam asked his brother.

"Start light," Trey responded, "enough to run fifteen, sixteen laps, see if I can get the lead, then fill up and go for the final push."

"You agree?" Adam asked Ethan.

"Sounds good to me," the crew chief said. "Probably the optimum approach, considering the field of drivers we're facing."

Ethan was ultimately in charge, but it was vitally important that the two men be on the same wavelength. Serious disagreements between a driver and crew chief presaged the end of a relationship. They had to be in sync for success.

Trey started in seventh position, not ideal, but not a bad spot to be in, either. The Daytona track was one of the two biggest on the circuit. Banking on the turns was steep, which facilitated speed. Carburetors had to be fitted with restrictor plates on these tracks to slow the cars down, but it didn't lessen the challenge. NASCAR racing wasn't just about speed; it was about skill in handling a car in a pack with forty-two other cars, all capable of going 180-plus miles an hour.

"You're in fifth," Ethan told Trey over the radio. "Time to pit."

Gas up and two-tire change took 13.69 seconds and Trey was again on his way.

Six laps later, just before the halfway point, Kent Grosso pitted, giving up his lead position. The thirtieth lap marked a major change in tactics. Till then the competition had been gentlemanly, now it turned predatory. Four cars had been eliminated because of engine or mechanical failures. Three others were lagging behind and were expected to drop out soon. That brought the field down to seventeen cars.

As Kent Grosso pulled off pit road and accelerated into Turn One, there was a wreck at the end of Turn Two. Kent jammed on his brakes, barely missed crashing into Jem Nordstrom and was about to veer right to pass him, when Trey Sanford cut around him on the outside.

For the next ten laps it became a battle between only two drivers, both of them dogged by Will Branch.

They were down to the last two laps.

TARA'S STOMACH was tied in knots. She'd cheered for teams and drivers hundreds, maybe thousands of times, but she'd never felt so personally involved in what was going on. She had no particular reason to want Kent Grosso to win. She wasn't exactly a personal friend of Trey Sanford's, yet she felt vested in him.

Because of Adam? Of course. And Kath and Brent. But she wasn't fooling herself. It wasn't even Trey. It was all about Adam, the team owner.

She watched him, standing atop the war wagon in the infield just behind the pit wall, more than she did the cars on the track. Tall, his broad shoulders emphasized by the team jacket he was wearing, his face half-hidden under the long-billed cap, he was still strikingly handsome, even from a distance. At least to her.

"White flag! One lap!" her mother was screaming. "Come on, Trey, goose it! Come on, baby, you can do it!"

Tara shifted her binoculars to the track. Trey and Kent were neck and neck, Trey on the outside. They went flying into Turn Three. Kent, on the bottom, was forced to back off slightly in order to keep from spinning out, but Trey, on the outside, had a longer distance to travel. At the top of the track between Turns Three and Four, they were parallel.

They flew into the last turn. The banking eased but didn't flatten out. They were in the gradual bend of the front of the D-shaped track. Both drivers had floorboarded their gas pedals. Kent, on the inside, veered right in an attempt to crowd Trey out. Trey held his ground. A crash now wouldn't do either of them any good. Kent eased back.

The checkered flag waved above them. Trey crossed the finish line less than a foot ahead of Kent.

VICTORY LANE was always sweet. It was what a driver raced for, what his team worked so hard to help him accomplish. With his arm around Adam's shoulder, Trey smiled at the cameras, nervously rubbing his chest with his right wrist before holding the trophy over his head and grinning like a kid on Christmas morning.

There were the expected interviews by the press, the standard poses with a variety of people for the media and the paparazzi, the usual autographs to sign—the hallowed rituals of winning.

Adam stepped back from the crowd that seemed about to swallow his brother. Trey was eating it all up, deservedly so. Adam rejoined the team that had made it happen.

"Thank you all," he said sincerely. "You guys are the best. I can't think of a better start for the season."

Finally he set out across the infield to his motor home. Dean Grosso was striding toward him, and to Adam's surprise, he was smiling.

"Congratulations," Dean sang out, his hand extended, as he drew closer. "Trey ran a terrific race today."

"Kent did, too. In the end it came down to luck."

"Luck and skill," Dean noted. "I've always believed skill makes our luck."

"Can I quote you on that?" Adam asked, baffled but relieved that there seemed to be no tension between them. They both knew the score. The end could have been reversed without anyone ever knowing why. That was the luck part.

Patsy came up from behind her husband and offered Adam her congratulations, as well. "Was Jake able to get hold of you?"

"No," Adam replied. He removed the cell phone from its belt holster. "I still have it turned off." He pressed the button to activate it.

"We don't need to be talking about this out here." Patsy motioned to their motor home, which was only a few yards away. Adam read the missed-calls list. Jake was third on it. Instead of listening to the voice mail, however, Adam slipped the instrument back into its carrying case.

Inside the motor home, the three of them gathered around the granite countertop that separated the kitchen from the living area.

"What's up?" Adam asked.

"Jake found out who leaked the story," she said sternly.

"It was so obvious," Dean observed with equal seriousness. "We should have been able to figure it out ourselves. Simple process of elimination. It wasn't Milo or Juliana, and it certainly wasn't Patsy or me."

"It wasn't Tara, either," Patsy added.

Adam waited.

"It was our new housekeeper. Clarice overheard Dean and me arguing…well, discussing what to do about trying to find Gina, and I guess she figured she had a gold mine. I hope she got well paid by the paper for the scoop, because she sure won't be working for us or any other NASCAR people, not after the way she betrayed our confidence."

"Does Tara know?" Adam asked.

Patsy grinned slyly. "We thought we'd let you tell her."

CHAPTER NINETEEN

ADAM BOLTED from the Grosso motor home. Where would Tara be? With her folks probably. And where would *they* be? Adam remembered their bright red motor home. It shouldn't be difficult to find, but not from ground level in the commotion produced by the mass of people maneuvering to leave the track.

He reversed course and knocked again on the Grossos' door. Dean answered with an inquiring expression, amusement playing on his lips. "Forget something?"

"Mind if I go topside?" Adam blurted anxiously. "I need to find the Dalton's motor home."

Patsy appeared behind her husband and nudged him aside. "The bright red one, right? It's in the southwest corner of the infield lot. When I talked to Shirley earlier today, she said they were staying for the race next week, so it should still be there."

Adam started to make a break for it.

Patsy grabbed his arm, stopping him. "Tara will put up a fight, you know. She'll resist you. So persevere."

He felt suddenly lightheaded. "Thanks." He winked at her. "I plan to, if it takes me the rest of my life."

Her face broke into a playful grin. "Good luck," she said, and let him go.

He leaped down the steps and thought he heard Dean say, "Attaboy," but he couldn't be sure. He dodged through the crowd.

Thanks to the security floodlights, he found the Dalton

motor home without difficulty a few minutes later. It stood out like a shiny red apple in a sea of weeds. Adam looked around. No sign of Tara or any of the members of her family. Probably all inside. The night air was damp and chilly, the kind that called for the warmth of another body.

Taking a deep, prayer-filled breath, he mounted the four metal steps, exhaled and rapped on the door. What seemed like an eternity elapsed, though it probably wasn't more than a few seconds before Buddy Dalton opened it.

"Hi, Adam," he said as if he was expecting him. "Great race tonight. Our congratulations to Trey. He's going to have a winning season, I can tell."

"Uh, thanks," Adam replied, trying hard not to reveal his impatience. "Is Tara with you?"

"She's right here," Shirley called out from behind her husband. She elbowed Buddy aside and practically shoved her daughter through the doorway at Adam. No sooner was Tara standing on the small platform at the top of the steps than the door behind her was slammed shut.

"We need to talk," Adam said only inches away.

She gazed up at him. They were so close he could touch her. It took all his self-control not to reach out, swallow her in his arms and kiss her passionately, but her blue eyes were hooded with suspicion.

"Please," he murmured.

"Oh, all right." She huffed with resignation, but Adam hadn't missed the gleam in her eye, the hunger lurking there, a reflection of his own.

"Let me grab a sweater," she said. "It's cold out here."

The words were hardly out of her mouth before the door behind her swung open and Shirley thrust a bulky, white sweater into Tara's hand, then closed the door firmly again.

Adam snickered in spite of himself. They would have to get away from the motor home, if they expected any privacy.

Tara shoved her arms into the sweater sleeves as she started down the steps. "What did you want to talk about?" she asked at the bottom.

He came up beside her, wanting desperately to put his arm around her, to offer his warmth in place of the sweater's, but he sensed the overture wouldn't be welcome; she wasn't ready. Or maybe he hadn't earned the right yet. If he persevered, though... Thrusting his hands into his pants pockets, he said, "I thought you might like to know who leaked the story to the newspaper."

"Who?" she asked immediately.

"The Grosso housekeeper, Clarice. She overheard them talking... Patsy fired her."

They walked on for a few more yards.

"How did you find out?" she asked.

"I hired Jake McMasters—"

"You hired him?" She glanced over at Adam. "Well, at least now you know it wasn't me."

"I never thought it was."

"Yes, you did." The contradiction was instant. He could hear the pain in it.

"I considered the possibility, Tara. Was that so wrong? Considering a possibility?"

"I guess not," she acknowledged. "Thank you for letting me know. I guess we ought to be getting back." She began to reverse course.

He stepped in front of her and blocked her way. "Not yet." He gently clasped her arms just below the shoulders.

Their eyes met. "What do you want, Adam?" she asked in a soft voice.

"To apologize for being such a damn fool. To ask your forgiveness for even having doubts. To beg you for another chance."

TARA'S HEART began to beat faster, harder. She couldn't believe she was hearing Adam Sanford, team owner, dominant male, the guy who was always in charge, being so contrite. He seemed so sincere.

She sighed. "Apology accepted." She resumed walking, not toward the motor home but in a continuation away from it, and it was more like a stroll than a stride now. "I guess I owe you an apology, too," she said. "I did a lot of things wrong, things that gave you justification for distrusting me. You have good reason to think journalists are lower than a snake's belly, and the way I acted reinforced all your negative concepts. I'm sorry."

"So can we start over again?" he asked. "Will you give me another chance?"

She stopped and faced him. "To what, Adam? We're so unalike. So incompatible. I mean…I'm a writer. You don't like writers."

"I don't like how some writers abuse their talents," he gently corrected her. "Some drivers cheat. That doesn't mean all drivers cheat. I had an unfortunate experience with one particular writer. What I'd forgotten was that I'd also read some very good books. One of them was *Rolling Uphill*."

She couldn't help smiling. "Flatterer." She resumed her perambulation.

He grinned at her. "Can't you handle a compliment?"

Where were they going with this conversation? she wondered. She soon found out.

"I love you, Tara," he declared, his head up, eyes straight ahead.

Her heart skipped a beat and her legs ceased their forward motion. She stared up at him, his back now a few feet ahead of her. "What did you say?"

He turned to face her. Even in the light of the distant flood-lights, she could make out the greenness of his eyes. "I said I love you." He closed the distance between them and took her hands in his. The warmth of his touch threatened to melt her. "You say we're not compatible. Maybe you're right, but I'm hoping you'll give us a chance to find out. There's so much we haven't explored, so many questions we haven't talked about. Like having kids."

"Kids?" She felt like a parrot repeating his words.

"You know, children. Babies. After we get married, of course. Personally I'd like to have a houseful of kids."

Love, marriage, children, family. She wanted to dance, to cry, to throw herself in his arms. She laughed. "I know what kids are, Adam."

"I love you, Tara, and I'm hoping you'll come to love me." He cupped the side of her neck. Instinctively she leaned into it.

"Enough one day to marry me," he said.

He kissed her on the forehead. He kissed her fleetingly on the lips. "I can promise you, I'll never be a Wild Bobby. I'll never be unfaithful to you."

She listened to his words, and she believed the heartfelt sincerity in them. She believed him. His marriage to Ashley had failed, but not because he'd been unfaithful. As far as she could tell, his ex-wife hadn't been unfaithful, either. They just hadn't been compatible, but wasn't that precisely the problem she and Adam had now?

"That's good to know," she acknowledged softly, "but it's not enough."

He stared at her and blinked. "Not enough?"

She heard anxiety and confusion in his voice. He'd just offered himself, body and soul, and she was saying it wasn't enough. "There's more than one kind of trust. You have secrets you're not willing to share with me."

He worked his jaw, his eye contact slipping, his brow furrowed in concentration. "You mean about Trey and his trips to Mexico."

She nodded.

He extended his elbow to her. She tucked her hand under it, coiled her fingers around the sinewy muscle of his forearm and rested it there. They walked side by side in silence for a few paces before he answered.

"Remember when we first met? You maintained that what was in the public domain was fair game?"

"Yes, I remember, but—"

"And I countered that what you may consider fair game I may regard as none of your business?"

"Yes," she replied, irritated by the reminder, "I remember."

"Some things are very personal, confidences we're not free to reveal. My brother's flights to Mexico fall into that category. For now I can tell you this. The trips and what he does there are all legitimate and honorable, but they are a deeply private matter."

"Is it about a woman? A child?"

The perplexed expression on his face baffled her. "I'm not at liberty to say. Only Trey can tell you. Can you let it go for now?"

She mulled it over. He was asking her to accept something on faith, after he had just pledged his fidelity to her. She'd accepted that vow. Now she had to decide if she was willing to concede that he had a right to keep his brother's secret from her, a secret about something he said was legal and honorable.

It didn't make sense, not on the surface. If there was nothing wrong with what Trey was doing, why couldn't Adam tell her about it? But there was another aspect to it. The right to privacy—Trey's privacy. Given the betrayals the family had endured—Kath by Wild Bobby, Brent by friends and associates, Adam by his ex-wife—Tara could understand why it was so important to him to maintain a confidence. She closed her eyes.

Give him a reason to trust you.

"Yes," she finally agreed. "I can respect that."

A broad grin swept across his face. "You still haven't answered my other question," he said. "So you'll give us another chance?"

She couldn't help but smile as her pulse thrummed. Giving *him* a second chance had suddenly become giving the two of them a second chance as a couple. The mistakes hadn't all been on his part. She'd committed her share. Overcoming them was something they would have to do together.

"Don't you want to ask me if I love you?"

"If you say yes, then you do, because you would never say yes if you didn't."

Amused, she crooked an eyebrow. "And if I say no?"

"Doesn't mean you don't love me. Well, it could. Or it could just mean that I have to work harder to earn your love, to prove to you that I love you." He slipped his arms around her waist. She gazed up at his handsome face, content to be exactly where she was. He lowered his mouth to hers and kissed her hard. "I love you, Tara," he murmured in her ear. "Don't ever doubt that."

"And I love you, Adam. Now," she added playfully, "can we go somewhere and get in out of the cold?"

He laughed. "I know a place, and it's not very far."

* * * * *

For more thrill-a-minute romances set against
the exciting backdrop of the NASCAR *world, don't miss:*
BLACK FLAG, WHITE LIES by Jean Brashear
Available in February 2009.
For a sneak peek, just turn the page!

ONCE WILL BRANCH HAD been her dream, but she'd been a girl then, naive and hopeful.

Zoe was neither of those now.

Will's eyes narrowed. "You have no idea who I am."

"That's right," Zoe shot back. "And I can't afford to trust you. Not with my child."

"My child, too." His voice was low but threatening.

"Biology doesn't make a father. It only makes you a sire. A father has to do a lot more."

"You think I don't know that? Me, of all people?" Then he straightened and took a deep breath. "How can I prove anything to you if you don't give me a chance?"

"Fatherhood is more than discussing video games."

A muscle leaped in his jaw. "That's right. It's also spending time together—"

"Until it's time to go be a driver again?"

"Damn it, Zoe, I'm trying to do the right thing. Get out of the way and let me do it."

"Out of the way? I'm his mother. I'm all he's got."

"No. Not anymore. Now he's got me."

His determined words, his solemn tone sent dread racing through her. "I should never have told you." She started to turn away, but he caught her arm.

"You won't keep him from me or my family. Not now, not ever."

"Is that a threat?" She held firm, though her legs felt like they'd collapse beneath her.

Will exhaled. Held up his hands. "This is getting way out of control." He stepped away. "I'd better go."

"I think you should."

He cast a glance down the hall where Sam had gone. "I want to tell him goodbye."

"I don't think so."

His eyes narrowed. "Don't push me, Zoe. I have the money to fight you, too."

Real fear clawed at her throat. "You wouldn't." Oh, God. This couldn't be happening.

"Mom? Is everything all right?" Sam's voice coming down the hall.

"I'm sorry." Will exhaled sharply, raked one hand through his hair. "I don't want to be at odds with you."

"Mom?"

She stared at Will, heart pounding, and called out to Sam. "Everything's fine, honey. Will was just leaving."

"He's going already?"

Will's gaze remained locked on hers for endless seconds as they both heard Sam's footsteps approach. The atmosphere shimmered with pain and fury, and Zoe was terrified of the future.

"Let's not do this," Will urged, his voice low. "For Sam's sake."

She closed her eyes then. Took a deep breath. What she wanted was to grab Sam, to run far and fast. But when she opened her eyes again, Will's expression was no longer hard but as confused as she felt. "I don't want to, either," she responded.

"I'll call you tomorrow. We'll work something out, okay?"

She nodded, but her chest remained tight.

As Sam entered, Will tore his eyes away at last. He dropped

to a crouch in front of Sam. "I wish I could stay, but my brother's coming in today, and I have to pick him up at the airport."

Sam shrugged. "It's okay." But he sounded disappointed.

"Maybe we could all three get together soon," Will suggested. "Bart would like you, too."

She watched Sam's eyes grow wistful at the notion that Will liked him, but he was far too cautious a child to assume anything. Her own eyes stung at the evidence of how much Sam needed a father, how much he craved a man's attention and approval. *You had better not hurt my child, Will Branch. Or I will make you pay.*

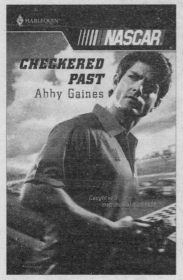

REQUEST YOUR FREE BOOKS!

2 FREE NOVELS PLUS 2 FREE GIFTS!

SPECIAL EDITION®

Life, Love and Family!

YES! Please send me 2 FREE Silhouette Special Edition® novels and my 2 FREE gifts (gifts are worth about $10). After receiving them, if I don't wish to receive any more books, I can return the shipping statement marked "cancel." If I don't cancel, I will receive 6 brand-new novels every month and be billed just $4.24 per book in the U.S. or $4.99 per book in Canada, plus 25¢ shipping and handling per book and applicable taxes, if any*. That's a savings of at least 15% off the cover price! I understand that accepting the 2 free books and gifts places me under no obligation to buy anything. I can always return a shipment and cancel at any time. Even if I never buy another book from Silhouette, the two free books and gifts are mine to keep forever.

235 SDN EEYU   335 SDN EEY6

Name	(PLEASE PRINT)

Address	Apt. #

City	State/Prov.	Zip/Postal Code

Signature (if under 18, a parent or guardian must sign)

Mail to the Silhouette Reader Service:
IN U.S.A.: P.O. Box 1867, Buffalo, NY 14240-1867
IN CANADA: P.O. Box 609, Fort Erie, Ontario L2A 5X3

Not valid to current subscribers of Silhouette Special Edition books.

Want to try two free books from another line?
Call 1-800-873-8635 or visit www.morefreebooks.com.

* Terms and prices subject to change without notice. N.Y. residents add applicable sales tax. Canadian residents will be charged applicable provincial taxes and GST. Offer not valid in Quebec. This offer is limited to one order per household. All orders subject to approval. Credit or debit balances in a customer's account(s) may be offset by any other outstanding balance owed by or to the customer. Please allow 4 to 6 weeks for delivery. Offer available while quantities last.

Your Privacy: Silhouette is committed to protecting your privacy. Our Privacy Policy is available online at www.eHarlequin.com or upon request from the Reader Service. From time to time we make our lists of customers available to reputable third parties who may have a product or service of interest to you. If you would prefer we not share your name and address, please check here. ☐

SSE08R